CU00498910

To Claire,

Thank you so much for
your support!
    Happy reading!
    Love, Sonia
        XO

Papillon

Copyright © 2023 by Sonia Palermo

All rights reserved.

Book Cover by Graphic Escapist

Editing by Charlie Knight cknightwrites.com/editing

CONTENT NOTE

Some content within this novella may be disturbing or triggering for some readers. Reader discretion is advised.

Subjects include mental illness, parental loss (off page/past), postpartum psychosis (off page/past), self-immolation (off page/past), suicide, self-harm (cutting), self-harm (burning), drowning (on page), alcohol and drug use, smoking, mention of foster care, medically-induced coma, graphic sexual scenes, BDSM, and strong language.

Any character depicted in a sexual scene is at least 18 years of age.

This book should not be used as a reference or guide for safe BDSM practices. Kinks include erotic degradation and humiliation, exhibitionism, praise, spitting, breeding, katoptronophilia, CNC, stalking, somnophilia, blood play, and impact play.

To the ones who embrace their darkness.
Stay metal.

1

MILLIE

JUNE 20, 2012

My world ended long before 2012 began.

Before the promise of apocalypse. Before I had my first drink. Before I smoked my first joint, had my first kiss, first fuck. Probably before I was even born.

The doctors said it was suicide that killed my mother. It wasn't. Every cause has effect. Suicide was the effect—not the cause—of why she doused herself in petrol and sparked a match when I was less than one month old.

I don't remember being burned, but the raised, uneven tissue that runs up my right leg, where I was too close to the fire, and the scars in my DNA prove it was real. And now I'm bound to the same ill-fated end.

Everything about this forsaken life has been one long, fucked-up ride. And I'm far from willing to hang around to see how the next twenty-three years pan out. I don't really want to die, but I can't keep living like this.

I suck in a breath as deep as my lungs and the crisp sea air will allow. Daytime in June on the south coast of England is usually sunny and warm, but the temperature drops as soon as the sun goes to sleep. My bones have felt cold forever. I throw my hood up and zip my jacket all the way to the top. The black moon mirrors my heart as dark waves lap dark sand, wiping away all traces of what's been there before. Poetry in motion.

I was born in a bathtub during a storm, and this sleepy seaside town has been my home for my entire life, so it makes sense that the ocean is where I'll live out my final moments, that I'll get to take my first and final breaths underwater. And maybe I've romanticised my death far too much, but I've been trapped in a glass jar for longer than I care to admit. I should be allowed to have something just for me, right?

I check the time on my phone; 22:22. Soon, it will be pitch dark. But I've made good time. I finished work at 5pm, went home to my one-bedroom flat, cleaned, showered, ate, drank a couple of vodka tonics, and pre-rolled some joints for the road—though I doubt I'll need them; it was never my plan to be shitfaced, just brave enough to carry this through.

Perhaps it's taken me twenty-three years to truly appreciate a beautiful sunset, but tonight, I savour it like it was meant for me—a prologue to the beginning of my end. I light a joint and take a hit. How bittersweet that this is the last time I'll taste anything else other than the saltwater of the wide-open ocean, that the setting sun would pave my journey into the dark. But I've always thought drowning seemed like a peaceful way to go.

There are things I'll miss. Like the smell of freshly cut grass in the peak of summer, or the pleasure of walking past someone who smells so good you want to ask what perfume they're wearing. The first leaves of autumn, the earth after rain. But it's not enough. Scents and changing seasons aren't a valid reason to stay here. No one gets out of here alive, so why should it matter how and when we decide to leave?

2

ZAIN

One in ten looked-after children are reported missing every year. I am the one in ten. Or, rather, the body I share is.

Zain Hawkins was seventeen years old and drinking himself into an early grave when he ran away from a care home. When he returned a month later, he wasn't the same boy. I guess by society's standards, I'm a monster for being a soul-swapping body snatcher. But what I'm really doing is giving these humans a second chance at life. It's easy to occupy someone else's body when the people around them don't give a shit about truly knowing them.

Some might say that being an empath is a blessing; others call it a curse. Sure, I've seen both sides—being one myself. I've seen all its ugliness, but when it's beautiful, it's glorious. For millennia, I've collected, nurtured, and prepared lost souls to be reborn, and the one cardinal rule of being the God of Death? Never fall in love with a mortal.

I've never been in danger of that happening. First of all, I don't stay in this dimension long enough to catch feelings, though that doesn't mean I don't fuck around with humans—if you get my drift. Secondly, I take my job very seriously. Before I inhabited my current body, I was a forty-five-year-old aspiring cross-fitter. But spending six months of the year in the underworld wreaked havoc with my earthside spartan mindset. It was tough keeping up appearances, and I got bored of the discipline, so I gave the guy a heart attack. Poor bastard was ready to go, or so I tell myself.

The best thing about being in a younger body? I still age, but I don't notice it half as much. No aches or pains—unless you count muscle soreness from hitting PB's at the gym. I go to work, eat my greens, look after my liver most of the time, and browse dating apps. Anyone would think I'm your average red-blooded, twenty-five-year-old, human male. Damn, mortals really are easy to fool.

Tonight, the moon is dark, but stars illuminate the sky, and the ocean glitters in waves as they crash against the shore. I breathe in the crisp sea air, tuck my journal under my arm, and lean against the rail of the pier.

And I watch her. The strange beauty.

I've watched her for nine years, through every failed attempt at ending her life. The first time, she slit her wrists in the bath. I waited for her, but I knew she wasn't meant for me that day. Her cuts weren't nearly deep enough for a start, and less than an hour of her pretty blood marbling the water, her mother forced her way in after finding her suicide note.

Millie's romanticisation of suicide is pathetic but vaguely amusing, and more endearing than I care to admit. Over the years, I've seen her grow from an ordinary, colourless girl to a rare creature of delicate, exquisite beauty. She's one of the reasons why I chose this vessel—I would never normally inhabit someone so young, but I highly doubt she'd look twice at someone three times her age. She's the one thing I want, and the one thing I can't have. Maybe it's the new moon, maybe it's sheer coincidence, but tonight, I sense a change in the air.

I check my watch. It's 22:22. The perfect time for endings, beginnings, and breaking the rules.

3

MILLIE

B elieve me when I say I've tried to get the notion out of my head that there's more to life than simply existing. Like most people, I have good and bad days, but in the end, the bad outweighs the good. Sometimes, waking up is a chore, and even on my good days, I can sense the demons lurking. Like clockwork, their whispers turn to roars, and there's nothing I can do to silence them. They killed my mother, and now they've come to kill me, too. And tonight, they'll succeed.

I know I have people who love me, people I'd hurt indefinitely if I ended things. But my parents, although I love them dearly, aren't my parents. And I can't ignore the call of my blood mum. Of death. Of losing my breath in an infinity of glittering waves crashing against my chest, silencing my pain, dulling the ache that I've carried in my heart for the last twenty-three years. I just hope they can forgive me.

The water comes closer. But it's not time yet.

I unzip my backpack, reach inside, and pull out a wooden box. Starlight guides my vision as I trace my finger across intricate carvings of daisies and moons in all their lunar phases as I lay it on the shingle in front of me.

Carefully, I lift the lid and find an opening in the purple velvet which holds my mother's tarot cards, slowly unravelling the cloth until the deck is in my hands. They're large and awkward to handle, but I like the way they feel. I don't pretend to know what they mean—I was never left a manual, and I've never taken the time to study tarot. But sometimes, I think I can feel her energy through them. Like when I hold them, I feel closer to her. It's a small feat of comfort, but I'll take it.

I sit awhile, holding the cards and being with my thoughts as I try my best to shuffle them. As a direct result of my awkward handling, two cards fall from the deck onto my lap. I take it as a sign and turn them over; The Devil and Death.

It seems fitting for the situation. Taken literally, the eternal pessimist in me would interpret those two cards as I'm going to meet my death at the hands of the devil. Or, in my case, the demons who currently live rent-free in my mind.

Carefully, I wrap the cards and place them back in their casing, which seems pointless, really, because they'll be at the bottom of the ocean in less than ten minutes if I can pull this off. I consider leaving them—saving them for someone else to find, but just like she was with me when I was born, I want her with me when I die.

I check the time again, but it doesn't register. In my periphery, a shadow comes towards me. I turn towards the shadow, and at first, I think it's a hallucination. But as the dark, blurry mass draws closer, I can make out the silhouette of a tall, slim figure. They're walking along the shore, boots ankle-deep in water. I'm aware that I'm holding my breath as the shadow comes into focus, but I'm frozen, mostly through curiosity but also fear. A violent wave crashes against my feet, jolting me back to reality, and my lungs deflate.

Wouldn't it be just my luck if my face ended up in the papers tomorrow? If, after all this planning, I end up being a fucking murder victim. I can see it now, my Facebook profile picture plastered over the news for people to fawn over. Local woman missing. Young professional found dead.

That poor girl.

No. I won't let that happen. If I'm going to die tonight, it will be on my terms, not because of some dollar-store creep who's watched too many slasher movies. The last thing I need is for some psychopath to finish me off when I have a carefully crafted suicide note written out. What a fucking waste of my time that would be.

I hold my breath again when the shadow comes within touching distance. It's too dark to see their face, but I can see that their boots are wet, and the thought crosses my mind that it's an incredibly strange thing to be walking in water with shoes on—even though my plans for the evening go a little more extreme than that.

"It's a pretty bold move to approach a stranger when it's dark," I deadpan in an attempt to save face. "Can I help you with something?"

"Don't put down your guns yet, Papillon," the shadow says.

What an odd thing to say.

He turns and gestures toward the direction he came from. "I was just taking a walk." His voice is soft, with a slightly rough undertone, like someone with a bad habit—not that I'm one to talk. With the glow of the pier behind him, I can see his face a little better. Oddly, I don't feel threatened, but I keep my guard up anyway. "I saw you over here, and I just wanted to see if you were okay. It's not very often I see people around at this time of night. Can I ask...what you're doing out here by yourself?"

Oh, nothing. I'm just about to throw myself into the ocean. No big deal.

"Just watching out for weirdos. You?" I ask, hoping that my loose translation of *kindly, fuck off* gets through to him.

"Same," he deadpans.

"Joke's on you—I'm one of them."

"Oh, so am I." Shingle crunches under black, heavy boots as he perches beside me.

"What are you doing?" I was feeling pretty smug before he showed up to impose on my plans, but now I'm irritated. I thought my disinterest would inspire him to leave, but it seems to have had the opposite effect.

"Getting comfortable, what's it look like?"

A soft breeze carries his scent towards me—he smells like a hipster's herb garden, woodsy and aromatic. It's dizzying but warm. And it's actually kind of nice. The stars illuminate his face, and I can distinguish a straight nose and sharp jaw hidden behind dark, shoulder-length hair. He reminds me of one of those book heroes, like a younger Aragorn or an older Prince Caspian. My fear dampens slightly because hot guys can't be serial killers, right? That's probably not entirely true if Billy Loomis and Patrick Bateman are anything to go by.

"Do you have a name, good samaritan?" I ask so I can at least know who my killer is.

"Zain." He flashes a disarming smile.

Heat spreads to my cheeks, then travels down...down and roots itself deep in my belly. My automatic response is to stare at the ground in an attempt to compose myself, but it doesn't work as well as I hope it does. I sneak another glance toward him while he stares at the ever-nearing tide. No, way too cute to be a psychopath.

"What you got there, Zain?" I ask as I gesture towards something that looks like a notebook tucked under his arm.

He snaps his gaze to it like he'd forgotten all about it. "Oh. It's my journal."

"Is that so you can keep a log of your victims?" I blurt. I can't believe I said that out loud.

"That's a strange way of asking if I'm a serial killer." He disarms me again with a raised eyebrow and lopsided smile, but he sobers almost instantly. "I'm not, by the way. And even if I was, you haven't given me your name yet."

"Hmm. I'm pretty sure I've seen this movie," I say, playing along with a wry smile.

Oh my God, am I flirting?

"How about I give it a guess?" he asks.

"I dare you."

His gaze turns darker, menacing. "Okay, cocky. If I guess your name right in three tries or less, you come home with me."

Well, that was unexpected. I'm shocked that someone could be so forward, yet I'm surprised at the sudden rush of adrenaline racing through me.

"And what if I win?"

"I'll leave you alone, or..." He pauses. "Come home with me anyway."

I shouldn't be thinking that this is the hottest thing anyone's ever said to me, and I definitely shouldn't be seriously considering his offer, but I do. Maybe it was the delivery, but that line sparked something deep in my belly and a warmth between my thighs. And, weirdly, I find myself trying to communicate my name via telepathy.

I've never had a one-night stand. It's not that I'm against them; I've just never been presented with the opportunity before. Although a quick reflection on my dating history is basically a series of one-night stands with the same person multiple times until we both get bored and ghost each other. But if a one-night stand is what Zain is proposing, it might be just the thing I need to tick off my bucket list.

4

MILLIE

"Then why not skip the guessing?" I say, astounded by my boldness. I can tell he's a little taken aback, too, but his serious expression doesn't falter.

"There's a time and a place to play dirty, Papillon."

My stomach flips. How does this guy manage to master two equally hot lines without breaking a sweat while I'm over here, crossing my legs and squirming over a few words?

"I'm going to try and guess now if that's okay with you?"

I nod.

"Look at me. I need to see your eyes," he commands. And I do. But I'm not sure how long I'll last without squirming again.

"A, b, c," he says the letters of the alphabet slowly. Measured while he casts his gaze over my face. "H, i, j." I'm not sure what he's doing exactly, but I'm intrigued to see where this will go. "K, l, m, n." He pauses suddenly. "Your name starts with an M?"

Fuck. Something in my expression must have given that away.

"How did you...?" I can't even bring myself to finish the question.

"Magic." He flips open the book, pulls out a pen from its holder, and writes down the letter M.

"A, b, c, d." This time, I try to keep my expression as neutral as I can, but the more I try to concentrate on not giving the game away, the harder it becomes. "E, f, g, h, i..." He pauses again and marks down the letter I. Damn, I suck at this. This is going to be easier for him than I thought.

"Miranda."

I shake my head and smile.

"Bummer."

"Is that a guess?" I ask, raising a brow.

"Strictly off the record. And kudos to anyone named Bummer," he says. "Okay, so I'm going to guess...Mildred?" His smirk leaves me wondering if he's just openly forfeited a guess and why.

"Close enough," I say, mirroring his expression.

When he pins me with his gaze, I sober. With the lack of light, it's hard to make out the exact colour of his eyes, but I can tell they're fair; some shade of green or grey or blue—not boring brown like mine.

"Millie."

"Bingo." I say it so quietly I question whether the words even left my mouth. But his smile indicates that he heard it.

"Pretty," he muses as he etches the rest of my name in ink.

"Thank you."

"You got a middle name?"

"Lua."

"Like the Portuguese word for moon. I like it," he says.

"I wouldn't know," I say. "I don't speak Portuguese."

"I'm a little rusty, I guess. My French is better."

He flashes that lopsided smile again, and my heart jumps a little.

I'm intrigued. I don't think I've met anyone who can speak another language, let alone two. Then again, I haven't met many people.

I clear my throat and turn my attention back to the journal. "What else do you write in there, other than your victims' names, Mr Serial Killer?"

"Intentions, observations, rituals..." he trails off.

"Rituals? Like Satanic rituals?"

The Devil.

He laughs, and suddenly I feel ridiculous. The sound is light. Warm. And nothing like how I would imagine the Devil's laugh to be.

"More like a ceremony. There's a new moon tonight."

I stare at him blankly. That witchy shit means nothing to me.

"Sorry, you don't have a clue what I'm talking about, do you? It's okay. Most people don't."

"How did you guess?"

"Your face, damn fucking cute as it is, gave it away." He turns his gaze toward the ocean, and I question if he's just regretted telling me that or if he's embarrassed because I'm pretty certain my cheeks are a hideous shade of crimson right about now. "Anyway. In short, I'm not a Satanist. I do, however, dabble with tarot from time to time," he says once he clocks the wooden box on my lap and the two fallen cards.

"I have no idea what they mean," I'm quick to say as if I'm ashamed of having them with me.

"May I?" he asks.

I nod, and he takes the opportunity to pick up one of the fallen cards. I say nothing, waiting to gauge his reaction, but his poker face is truly impressive.

"Ah, The Devil." He says it with familiarity, like it's an old friend, and I can't work out if he actually knows tarot or if he's fucking with me. He cracks his knuckles, and I catch a glimpse of the tattoos on his hands. I want to trace my finger along every line. I want to know what he feels like. "The Devil is your shadow side. It's everything that's buried in the wells of your subconscious. Fear, expression, desire, attachments. Those wonderful dark and negative elements of your psyche. The Devil is all the things that hold you back from doing what you really want. It holds you back from your deepest desires."

His gaze is darker than before but wild with a fire that threatens to burn holes into my retinas. If this is what he means by desire, then I guess the devil has me already.

He picks up the second card. "Death, despite what it is in the literal sense, actually represents rebirth and new beginnings. It's there to teach you what it means to be alive. It wants you to look death in the eye and say, 'come at me motherfucker.'"

I let out a tiny, pathetic laugh. And I think that maybe I've finally crossed the line of depression and descended into madness. I must be hallucinating. This Zain person...he's not real. He can't be. But I've got to give my imagination credit for conjuring up such a perfect specimen.

Maybe I'm already dead.

He reaches for the wooden box between my hands. "Mind if we do another?" he asks, and I don't put up a fight. The warmth of his fingers brings my skin to life and knocks the wind out of me when he prises it from my grasp. For a ghost, he feels incredibly real.

He unravels the cloth and shuffles with more ease than I'm capable of. "Pick a card," he says, offering me the deck. I pull one out and hand it to Zain.

"Two of Cups," he says. "Interesting." I wait for him to elaborate, but instead, he stands up and tucks the card into his back pocket and his journal under his arm. "I'm going to leave you to figure that one out, Papillon."

"Why do you call me that?"

"Papillon? It means butterfly."

I nod. "I know that, but why?"

He shrugs. "Butterflies can't see the colour of their wings."

Who is this guy, and why does he speak in fucking riddles?

"What is that supposed to mean?" I ask.

"It means that you have a future, despite how fucked up you might think you are. We're all broken, and you won't find the answers you're looking for at the bottom of the ocean." He walks away, his jarring words vibrating in my head, leaving me confused, speechless, and wanting answers.

"You're serious?"

He stops and turns, his face now too far to make out an expression. "What do you expect?"

"I don't know. Nothing," I say. I never expect anything from anyone. But all I know is the thought of being here alone again fills me with dread. "Five minutes ago, you were asking me to come home with you. What's changed?"

"Truthfully?" He pauses. "I didn't expect you to." His tone is soft yet confident and so casual and sincere that I'm instantly enamoured. He turns on the heel of those heavy black boots and walks away.

If I were sober, I might not have decided to follow him, but something inside me still calls the shots, telling me to test out his gravity. Maybe a part of me is still rooting for me.

"Do you want me to?" I'm surprised at my boldness.

Zain stops and turns to face me again. He's just as surprised as I am. Give a dog a bone, and they'll follow you forever. Or more like take a desperate loser's late mother's tarot card, and they'll follow you forever. "Yes. Yes I fucking do."

5

MILLIE

"Legend has it, the Pleiades were orphans who became stars because they weren't loved or cared for by the members of their tribe," Zain explains as we round a corner to a row of terraced townhouses. I don't know how long we've been walking, but every second has been accounted for in conversation about astronomy and stargazing and the other things he writes in that journal of his.

"That's heart-breaking," I say.

"But actually, sort of beautiful," he adds, reaching into his pocket and pulling out a set of keys. "They're forever immortalized." He leads me down the pathway of one of the houses to a bright red door, singles out a silver key with a rounded head, and turns it in the lock.

Zain walks in first, and I stand in the doorway feeling completely irresponsible. The only thing I know about this guy is that he looks like a god and has a penchant for stars and space. I'm on the sensible side of sober now—the brisk air and the walk

17

made sure of that, and now that all of this feels real, I'm trying to decide if I should follow him inside.

"You want something to drink? I make a mean cacao."

"Cacao?"

"It's basically a healthier version of hot chocolate."

"Sure," I say. My mouth is so dry I could drink anything right now. I shouldn't let that be a deciding factor to stay, but it is.

I follow him inside to a dark room dimly lit by the streetlights outside. He turns on a side light and places the journal on a dark wooden desk while my eyes adjust to my new surroundings.

A quick scan around the room tells me this guy has an un-healthy relationship with books; they're everywhere. Not that it's a bad thing, just...unusual for someone his age. I spot a TV mounted on the wall, some trinkets and well-used candles on the desk where his journal lays, along with a creepy-looking animal skull and a time-worn maroon Chesterfield covered in blankets and cushions.

"Make yourself at home," he says. After the night I've had, nothing looks more inviting than that hunk of leather. "Do you like music?"

"Doesn't everyone?"

I guess he meant it rhetorically because as I get the words out, he's already slipping a vinyl out of its sleeve and placing it on a record player. I don't think I've ever seen one of those up close. Again, a strange artefact for a twenty-something-year-old to have. He must be some kind of history buff. Either that, or he's one of those intellectual posers.

I sink into the sofa, bring my legs up and cross them over while I look for something to keep myself from fidgeting. I grab the cushion behind me, lay it in my lap, and play with a piece of frayed edging. I recognise the album as soon as it starts to play. Ocean Rain is one of my all-time favourites, next to Nevermind.

"You're a Bunnymen fan?" I ask.

"Since the beginning."

"But that would make you…" My brain tries to quickly do the maths, but it doesn't make sense. There's no way this guy is in his thirties.

He turns to face me, and I'm met with the brightest, bluest eyes I've ever seen. The kind that are so clear you can almost see right through them. God, he's beautiful. "Let's get you that drink. I'll be right back," he says before disappearing into the next room.

While he's gone, I take myself on a tour while my favourite songs play in the background. I forget how much music can make a person feel and forget and remember all at the same time. If this is my final evening on Earth, it's a pretty sweet way to go—unless I get a blunt object to the head; that would suck.

Books fill every shelf on almost every wall; medical textbooks, the occult, science, astrology, shamanism, mythology. Most of them so old I can barely make out the titles. I slide my fingers along the spines of dozens of journals, the pages beaten and used, exhausted, turned thousands of times. I pick one out and thumb through it; it dates back to 2002—the same year I was expelled from my shitty state school. Every entry is dated and beautifully handwritten in cursive, but it's difficult to make out the words with a lack of light. I put the journal back in its place and continue to explore.

Where there are no books, there's vinyl, and where there's no vinyl, there's candles, colourful rocks, gemstones, and vintage trinkets. My gaze lands back on that animal skull, but I still can't work out what it is or if it's even real, in the same way that I still can't seem to work out if any of this is real. I reach out to touch a horn, but a sudden noise throws me off my focus.

"I see you've met my pet."

I jolt, startled by Zain's presence. But when I turn to face him, my alarm dampens. He's holding two identical white mugs filled with something steaming. I could really use some warmth right now.

"Which one would you like?" he asks. I probably shouldn't be trusting strangers to make me drinks. But it's comforting that he's given me a choice. I go for the one on my right, cupping the mug in my palms. "Careful, it's hot."

That makes two hot things in this room.

Stop it, Millie.

"So, this is the famous cocoa?" I ask, knowing full well that he'll correct me. But he doesn't. Instead, he cocks a brow, his lips curving into a torturous smirk that sends a bolt of lightning straight to my stomach. It's uncomfortable and alien but weirdly addictive.

I clear my throat and turn my attention back to the so-called pet.

"Does your pet have a name?"

"Aries." Zain blows softly on his mug and takes a sip of his drink as the steam disperses across those perfectly full lips, and I can't help but imagine that face between my legs blowing on my soaking clit in the exact same way. Heat creeps between my thighs, but I shake the thought away before I get ahead of myself.

Jesus, Millie. What the fuck is wrong with you?

"Aries isn't very friendly," I say, finally striking up the nerve to touch the dry piece of bone. It's cool, smooth, a little chalky, and not completely offensive. In fact, it's kind of beautiful.

Zain shrugs. "I travel between jobs, so I'm away a lot. I'd love to have a *breathing* pet, but I can't afford that luxury. It wouldn't be fair on them to go to a sitter every time I'm away."

He takes another sip, and I follow his lead. The cacao tastes bitter like coffee and has a strong resemblance to chocolate, but without the sweetness. I take another sip to cement my opinion, but I'm not entirely sure how to feel about it yet.

"What do you think?" he asks.

"I... I'm not sure."

He laughs again. "It takes a bit of getting used to. I wasn't sure about it at first, but the benefits outweigh the weird taste." I feel like he should insert some kind of innuendo about blowjobs here, but he doesn't. And I'm a little disappointed that he didn't state the obvious while I'm left wondering what his dick tastes like. My eyes accidentally land on his crotch, but I avert my eyes quickly. He doesn't seem to notice. "Ceremonial cacao opens your heart chakra."

"Ceremonial?"

He takes another sip and sets the mug down on the desk behind him. "Come. You've got a lot to learn, Papillon." He offers his hand; I take it, and I'm instantly warmer. But he breaks contact as soon as we reach the couch. "Have a seat."

I do as he says, and he sits beside me. We face each other, and my paranoia sets in. Oh God, is this the part where I pass out? Did I get roofied? I search for signs within my body, but I feel the same as I did ten minutes ago. My mind may even be a little clearer.

"Are you going to kiss me?" I regret saying it the moment the words leave my mouth. What a ridiculous thing to say.

He's surprised but lets out a small laugh and shakes his head. "No."

"Oh." A lump gets lodged in my throat, and a feeling of dread settles in the pit of my stomach. "Are you going to fuck me?" God, I'm embarrassing. It's beyond me that I've managed to get this far in life, to be honest. *He won't fuck you if he doesn't even want to kiss you.*

"No," he deadpans.

He says it so coldly; I clench my thighs together. It's like I find pleasure in being humiliated. After a beat, his gaze darkens like a storm cloud moving over a clear blue sky, like he's enjoying

21

watching me squirm. "If and when I plan on fucking you, Papil lon... I need you to be in the right headspace. Sober. Understand that I will ruin you for anyone else." Heat spreads through my core and to every extremity, my head spinning with a cocktail of hurt, shame, lust, and an insatiable hunger that I can't place, falling somewhere between physical pangs, emotional, or both. "Until I say so, I won't even touch you. Understood?"

I turn my gaze to the mug in my lap, away from his inten- sity. I get it. He's right, of course. Even though I feel sober, my mental, physical, and emotional state is compromised, and there's nothing I want more than to have it fucked out of me, like the best kind of exorcism. He's probably just pretending to concern himself with my mental well-being, but I know better, and maybe if I try hard enough, I can convince him to change his mind.

"Okay," I drag out the 'a' like my life depends on it. "So, what am I doing here?" I'm not being completely delusional, am I? Everybody knows that inviting someone back to your place is generally code for sex.

He prises the mug from my hands and sets it atop a pile of books on a side table. I don't think I could stomach anymore. If anything, it's making my mouth drier, so I'm grateful for the reprieve.

"It's no coincidence that you and I met tonight, Millie." Okay, so this is the part when I get bashed over the head with a lamp or something. "Remember when I said I travel a lot for work?"

I nod.

"Well, I sort of heal people."

"What are you, God?"

He laughs. "Kind of." For an uncomfortable amount of time, all he does is look at me, and it feels like his eyes are reaching right into my soul. This is something that should feel awkward, but it doesn't. "I want to help you."

So that's what this is. He's not the big bad devil; he's a good Samaritan with a saviour complex. No, thank you.

The lump in my throat pushes down, making me nauseous. "Thank you, but I don't need a pity party."

It could be anyone holding a mug of this ceremonial bullshit; I don't matter in this equation. Why did I ever think otherwise? He's just some guy ticking a box on his good deed. I rise to leave, but he halts me by the arm.

"Wait, where are you going?"

"To do what I set out to do." I try to speak with conviction, but inside, I'm doubting my decision. I tug my arm away, grab the wooden box housing my mum's tarot cards and start toward the door.

"Millie." Zain's tone is serious. Authoritative. Like he's saying *don't you dare leave.* My hand hovers over the handle, maybe because a small part of me is hoping to be saved, another part knows I can't be, and the other won't let my body leave without hearing what he has to say.

"I know what you were planning to do tonight. And I didn't intervene to try and take your autonomy away, but it's a momentous waste of a life. Ask yourself this. If you really wanted to kill yourself, wouldn't you be halfway down the street by now?"

It's not like there isn't always that doubt in my mind when I do this. I don't think anyone who sets out to end their life is one hundred percent sure all the time. But all I know is nothing has changed since I started having these scary, heightened emotions. Since I found out the truth about my mum.

"Believe me when I say things will *always* get better." His voice comes closer. "Yours is a soul worth saving." Suddenly, his hand is on mine, slowly guiding it away from the handle, guiding me away from the outside world. "Come on, you know I'm right."

If I have to question whether or not he's right, he probably has a point. I retreat from the door and face him. "If years of therapy and medication can't help me, what do you do that's so exceptional?"

"Let's just say my methods are a little...unconventional. I need to work with your energy, and then we can decide on the next steps," he says mirthlessly. In the beat of silence that follows, my tummy takes the opportunity to make the most un-flattering sound. The weed has clearly worn off and manifested into hunger, and I know it hasn't gone unnoticed when he raises an eyebrow. "But first, you need to eat."

6

MILLIE

After finishing off the remnants of my lukewarm cacao, I wolf down two slices of toast with butter and jam, a bowl of fruit salad, and a couple of handfuls of mixed nuts. I could easily finish the entire contents of Zain's fridge, but I don't want to be greedy.

"You know staring is rude, right?" I say in an attempt to distract myself from the intensity of his intimidating gaze.

"Shh," Zain says. "I'm thinking."

I struggle to compose myself, especially when the person I'm looking at has the kind of face I could stare at for hours. If that makes me a hypocrite, then so be it.

"Will you stop smirking?" He's composed and serious, but there's a tiny glint in his eye that's almost undetectable. Then, his posture straightens up, as though he's found what he's looking for. "Okay, lie down." He rises from the sofa and lets me get comfortable, placing a cushion underneath my head.

"Think of this as initiation."

"Initiation? Are you part of a cult? Am I being sacrificed or recruited?" I'm mostly joking, but the tiniest part of me—the part of me that's had a wariness of men ingrained in me since girlhood—is a little anxious.

"Focus, Millie. Close your eyes, clear your mind, and listen to my voice. I'm going to feel your energy now, okay?"

"Okay."

I hear a click, and after a moment, a sweet, woody aroma mixed with something that smells remarkably like weed dances around my nostrils.

"Take five deep breaths and allow your mind and body to relax."

I do as he says, sinking a little deeper into the sofa with every exhale. My heartbeat slows, my body goes loose, my mind clears.

"I'm going to say some colours, and I want you to visualise that colour when I say it. Ready?"

"Yes."

"Red."

Images of fire and blood run through my mind. Warmth gathers between my legs. The feeling is so strong that it's almost like he's touching me. But then I remember his rule of no contact and tell myself that he's doing this purely to stop me from ending my life. Despite my first thoughts, he's not interested.

"Orange."

As soon as the word leaves his lips, images of sunsets and autumn leaves crunching on the ground flash through my mind. The imaginary glow spreads upwards towards my navel. I chase it with my hand and capture the spark as it nestles in just below my belly button. I've been cold for so long that wanting to contain every inch of warmth that befalls me seems like a natural progression.

He continues to name every colour of the rainbow, while heat travels all the way up my body, wraps itself around me, and seeps into my skin. My mind is saturated with yellow daffodils, lush green lawns, a clear blue sky, verbena flowers, amethyst.

In my mind's eye, I'm standing barefoot in a field of wildflowers wearing a white gown. I can smell the sweet, bitter grass and the crisp, floral notes in the air. My belly is warm, my heart, my throat, my brows, the crown of my head; they're all flowing with energy. I continue to chase the glow with my hand, but it's hard to stay focused when the warmth between my legs is growing stronger by the minute.

"Where are you, Millie?"

"In a meadow."

"Good girl. Keep going," he says, and in my fantasy, I turn to follow his voice. He's there, shirtless and barefoot. His smooth, pale skin is so beautiful I almost can't stand it. I want nothing more than to reach out and touch this angel who showed me mercy. He starts to softly chant the same word repeatedly. "La m...Lam...Lam...."

I don't know what it means, but when he says it, I point my gaze towards the ground and bury the soles of my feet in the damp grass, soaking up the cool dirt, and the soft, pulpy texture of the earth. It feels wonderful.

"Vam...Vam...Vam..." he chants, keeping to the same tempo as before.

Our eyes meet, and the only thing I want to do is put my hands on him. Instinct takes over and I reach out, tracing my fingertips down his sternum. Rainbows fall from my fingertips, leaving marks as I draw along every curve, every striation of muscle, his abs, the dip in his chest, every carving of that wonderfully sculpted torso, and finally the V-shaped lines that form a trail to his waistband. I don't stop until he resembles a human paint-by-numbers.

"It's okay," he says. "Keep going."

My fingers dip below his waistband, a kaleidoscope of colour seeping through my fingers, bleeding onto his skin and his black skinny jeans as I pull him towards me. And I kiss him. I kiss him like the last few hours haven't been a total mind fuck. I kiss him until I feel the earth shift between my toes and ground me into his gravity. I swear if I opened my eyes, I'd see leaves dancing around us like we're in some kind of fairy tale.

"Millie," he breathes.

His hand slips between my thighs, his touch warm and golden and hungry.

"Oh, God." Is this real? I can't help but feel like I'm falling into some deep, black hole. Like I'm spinning out of control and we're just a tangle of hands and breath and erratically beating hearts. It's the first time I've felt anything in...I don't know, a while.

He lifts my dress and pushes my underwear aside, then slides his finger along my pussy and presses a finger inside while his thumb lazily circles my clit. Every inch of me is aching for him.

"Zain." I call his name in an attempt to offset the ache, but it does the opposite, serving as a catalyst for my hunger.

"That's it. Show me how you touch yourself."

His words trigger a reaction within me, and suddenly the apparition is gone. *He* is gone, and I'm alone, standing in a field with bare feet and a white dress, with my fingers in my pussy, covered in mud and rainbow-hued bodily fluids, and riding on the edge of an orgasm. The fantasy dissolves, turning into vapour.

As soon as reality registers, I stop. Bile rises in my throat when I realise that I've just been fucking myself on a stranger's couch because of some Jedi mind trick he's pulled. And the worst thing of all? I didn't even get to finish.

"What the hell just happened?" I press my thighs together in an attempt to offset the ache from a lack of stimulation. My eyes are still closed when I pose the question. I won't dare open them. I hate to admit it, but I've never been so ashamed of myself.

"Congratulations. You've opened your root chakra," Zain says softly. "How are you feeling?"

"Thirsty."

"That's to be expected. You did good."

"You're not horrified?" I finally gather the courage to open my eyes. When I do, I'm met with those clear blue eyes. They calm me instantly.

"It's all part of the process."

If this is the beginning, I'm curious to see how it ends. There's no point in holding back now. I've already crossed a line.

7

MILLIE

JUNE 21, 2012

    I wake at 3am. Alone, but warm. Memories of last night, of candles flickering and the scent of lavender and rosemary on the pillow I lay upon, are my only form of company in the darkness, but I fall back to sleep before I have a chance to dwell on it or question last night in its entirety.

The next time I wake, sunlight streams through the windows, and I'm no longer by myself. As I rouse, my awareness brings me to Zain. He's perched on the opposite side of the bed with his back facing me, his shirtless body bathed in golden light. My gaze travels from the mass of dark hair on his head to where it ends just above his shoulder blades while my mind commits every inch of muscle definition to memory as I admire the work of art before me; a beautiful and fierce-looking warrior woman with wings that span the entire width of his back.

An angel who wears an angel.

As if he can hear my thoughts, Zain turns around. "Good morning, Papillon," he says, handing me a glass of water. Those beautiful, pale eyes are softer in the morning light but still completely captivating.

"Morning." My voice sounds nothing like the one I know. I take the glass and sip. Water has never tasted so good.

Suddenly, I'm aware of reality. Of the dryness in my mouth and the taste of stale weed and stale booze. There's no doubt in my mind that half of my makeup has ended up on the pillow, my skin no longer glowing but blotchy and uneven. My hair is a mess from being whipped around by the sea air. I wish I could wake up looking like those perfect girls on TV. Maybe when I'm dead, I'll get to wake up perfect every day.

"How did you sleep?"

"As cliché as it sounds, I slept like a baby." I don't even have to think about it; it's the best night's sleep I've had since I can remember. I don't want to jinx anything, but sleeping with the absence of nightmares is a novelty that I could get used to.

Zain looks at me like he's waiting for me to elaborate, but I don't want to bore him with the story of my recurring bad dreams.

"Can I make you some breakfast?"

As if on cue, my tummy makes an unattractive gurgling noise, pulling me out of my thoughts and giving me the sign that I need to remind myself that I am, in fact, still alive. I'm pretty sure dead people don't get hungry.

"You don't have to...I don't want to put you out..." I trail off.

"Millie." He pins me with his gaze the moment he says my name. "Let me make you some fucking breakfast." If those words fell from anyone else's mouth, I would have told them to stick their breakfast up their ass. But when Zain says it, calm and authoritative, it makes my pussy throb.

31

"Yes, Master," I say, with a touch more sarcasm than seriousness. But as soon as I say it his gaze turns stormy, like I've struck a nerve.

"Good." He schools his expression to neutral. "I'll be right back." He retreats to the kitchen while I take another sip of water, then I leave the glass on the bedside table before laying back down and pulling the covers up to my chin. "And wipe that smirk off your face."

If anything, I'm smiling harder.

8

ZAIN

"Your ass belongs to me now." I flash a sardonic smile and bite my lip.

The flash of fiery want in those pretty brown eyes doesn't go unnoticed.

Millie's enjoying her breakfast—a bowl of rainbow fruit salad full to the brim with superfoods—a little too much. And I'm here for it. It gives me immense pleasure to watch her enjoy something that I made for her. Almost as much pleasure as I got from watching her touch herself last night. But I'm trying not to think about that too much.

I spent most of the night watching her sleep, thinking the dirtiest of thoughts, wishing I could keep her as my pet so I could stroke her in the middle of the night, rousing that soft body awake with my hands, her sleepy voice breathy and wanting, saying my name in the way that she does. That earthy, sweet, addictive scent as she grinds her body slowly against my hand while the other one cups her breast, rolling those perfect, pink nipples between my fingers...

Never have I craved a human like this.

"Why are you looking at me like that?" she says with a mouthful of pineapple.

Shit.

I shake my head in an attempt to shake away the daydream, but the juice that's threatening to fall from the corner of her mouth doesn't make my dick twitch any less because all I'm imagining is my seed dripping down that pretty chin of hers.

"You just...you look like you're really fucking enjoying that." I don't even try to hide my smile.

"I am." She catches the drip with her tongue, and I swear to the gods it's one of the sexiest things I've seen a mortal do. No, not any mortal. Her.

What is it with this girl? And why won't my dick quit?

"Come to solstice with me," I blurt out. I'm shocked at my own forthcoming.

She takes another bite of blueberries and cantaloupe before she answers. "What is that?" The sound of her speaking with her mouth full is enough to make my dick strain against my jeans. But I try to focus on the task at hand; convincing her to join me.

"It's a festival we celebrate to mark the official beginning of summer in the Northern Hemisphere. It's the longest day of the year." *And my last day on Earth for the next six months.*

"Where is it?"

"Stonehenge."

"Isn't that, like, really far?"

"It's around two hours from here."

"Oh." She continues to eat, not giving me an answer.

"I think it would be good for you."

She drops her fork into the bowl and meets my gaze. "Good for me? Do you really think some meditation, a bowl of fruit, and a road trip is going to cure me?" She takes another mouthful. "It's a sweet gesture, Zain. But it's not exactly realistic."

Man, do I hate it when people call me sweet.

"Keep on acting like a brat, and you'll get punished, Papillon. Now eat your breakfast like a good girl, and I might let you come before we leave."

She opens her mouth to speak, then closes it. I can't tell if she's angry, shocked, or disgusted. But her incessant pout tells me it's probably all three.

I'm not proud of my premature outburst, but I'm not sorry, either. She clearly isn't ready to meet the real me, and that's okay. I spent thousands of years perfecting restraint; celibacy, veganism, sobriety—all futile attempts to fit into a so-called social construct. Mortals will do anything to belong, to embrace whatever society deems normal. But repression makes small evils worse. It's better to embrace the darkness.

Millie finishes her breakfast in silence before disappearing into the bathroom. I listen for any sign as to what she may be doing in there. I hear the turn of a tap and the rush of running water. Cupboard doors open and close softly, but I can still hear them. My Spidey senses are idle, giving me no indication that she'll harm herself. I'm confident that she'll come around—these mortals always do. So, I pace the room and wait, although I can't help but wonder if I've read her wrong. What if the one thing I've been wanting all this time doesn't want me?

Maybe I can't save her.

I shake the last thought out of my head and remind myself that I'm the Lord of Death. I should be taking lives, not saving them. And I'll be damned if I don't get what I want before my soul departs tomorrow.

After half an hour, I try the door.

"Millie?"

I'm met with silence. Then the lock turns, and I take it as an invitation.

"Are you okay?" I ask once inside.

"I'm fine," she says. Her voice conveys no indication that she isn't fine, so why should I think otherwise?

A white, fluffy towel covers up most of her body, but my gaze is naturally drawn to the drops of dew that coat her bare shoulders and calves, kissing that golden skin. Damp hair sticks to her neck, and the scent of eucalyptus fills the room. Her back is turned, but I catch her gaze in the mirror above the basin she's standing in front of. I don't know how someone can make a towel look good, but she does.

"About what I said," I start. I'm not the grovelling type, but I don't want her to go. My pride will have to take a back seat this time.

"It's not about what you said." She turns to face me. I realise it's the first time I've seen her without makeup on. She's infuriatingly beautiful. But delicate, like a painting. It baffles me that such a creation in human form is possible. To think I could ruin her with one touch... "It's just..." She folds her arms, hugging the towel closer to her chest. "This thing is like cancer. It's a disease. Treatments might help some people, but not everybody is that responsive. I appreciate that you want to help me, but you can't. I'm a lost cause."

"You underestimate me."

"Do I?" She raises an eyebrow.

I step closer. "Look. I've been where you are." My fingers instinctively find the scars that run along my inner forearm. Technically they're not my doing—they were part of this body before I was. But I still hold the trauma, the memories. I still feel every emotion. "Last night, when we met, I knew you were different. Like me." I pause, letting my words sink in. "Your despair, your darkness... It's what draws me to you." Those eyes, black as a new moon, soften slightly. "But you're wrong. It's not cancer; it's fear. And if you let your fear rule you, it will compress and become cancerous. But you don't have to let it kill you. You have a choice to embrace who you really are. Without your darkness, you'll never see the stars."

"And you have the magic cure, do you?"

Her stubbornness is driving me wild, but I try to remain calm. "I don't claim to have all the answers. But I can show you another way. If you'll let me?"

"I don't know." She turns towards the mirror, gripping the sides of the basin like she's holding onto a lifeline, then meets my gaze through the reflection. "Maybe it's best I go home."

"Best for who?" I ask.

"I don't know, both of us, I guess. I don't know why I'm still here or what you want from me. But I'd rather you just be honest."

"You sure you can handle that?" Within moments I'm standing behind her. I'm aware that my height can be intimidating to some. And at the moment, I'm only familiar with my idea of her. But I know she's not afraid of me.

Her eyes glaze for a moment, and I catch the scent of her arousal, but she quickly straightens up, standing tall with her chin lifted and gaze cold like she's readying for a fight. Stubborn little thing.

"I can handle it."

Oh, darling. If only you knew.

"I want you to stay. Here. With me. I want to rip off that towel, spread your legs apart, and run my tongue over the backs of your thighs all the way up to your pussy. I want to bury it inside your tight hole until you scream my name and forget your own." Her eyes become saucers, and a quiet, breathy moan escapes that perfect heart-shaped mouth. It's my ultimate undoing. "I can smell your sweet little cunt from all the way up here, Papillon. And it would be a damn shame to let you leave without letting me taste you." Her scent and the wild look in her eyes are making me feral, but at this point, I'm past caring. "Is that honest enough for you?"

9

MILLIE

It's been seconds, but it feels like a lifetime has passed since either of us have exchanged a word. I can barely think in Zain's presence—especially when he's this close—let alone speak. All I can do is listen to the roar of my heart and the beat of his breath.

"But I thought you said—" I startle myself because I don't expect the words to fall from my mouth.

"That I wasn't going to touch you?" He's almost too quick for me. Like he knows exactly what I'm thinking. "Is it a problem that I want to?"

His fingers splay gently across my throat, his eyes never leaving my face as he peels the damp hair from my skin and wraps it in his hands. I lean into him, and he tugs it across my shoulder, his grip firm as he lays it down the centre of my back. His scent is warm, like a log fire burning in the darkest winter, fresh as a summer storm. Fire and water. And it's driving me wild.

"God, I want you." His fingers skirt the edge of the towel, and I fight every urge to press my hips back into his.

Usually, I would never do this kind of thing, but Zain has me spellbound. I drop the towel, letting it fall to the floor. His breath hitches, and it's the sexiest sound I've ever experienced. And it is an experience because he has me feeling things and wanting things I haven't wanted since... forever.

"Tell me what to do," I say.

His eyes catch fire, blue as night. A flame's reaction zone. "Show me how you touch yourself."

I switch my gaze, scanning every inch of my bare flesh. I hardly recognise myself. Maybe it's the soft daylight that filters through the bathroom window or the angel standing behind me, but today, my reflection is easier to tolerate. My hair is already half-dry, formed in lazy waves, my skin fresh and clear, my eyes lusty, vision hazy. Clouded, like a dream. Only I've never been so awake. So conscious.

I lay a hand across the soft skin of my belly, dragging my fingertips up towards my chest, entranced in the way my fingers caress the dip in my throat, the side of my neck, and splay softly across my throat. Zain is quiet and still, watching me with hooded eyes as I trace a line down to my pebbled nipple and take it between my thumb and forefinger, pinching and pulling, gently massaging, dividing my attention between both breasts before one hand descends downwards, and slips between my legs.

My fingers, slick with arousal, slide over my folds, then my clit, and I gasp, revelling in the relief. My heart is pounding. Not just from the thrill of having an audience or the sheer fact that I even get to breathe the same air as someone so devastating. No. This is the first time in my life that I've ever felt seen. And it's terrifying.

I push one finger inside, then two, my desperation voiced in a pathetic whimper as I take them out and massage my clit, alternating between the two and wishing, just wishing, there were two pairs of hands touching me.

Zain wraps his hand around my hair and gently pulls me towards him, tipping my head back. I close my eyes as my neck stretches out, graceful as a swan.

"Eyes on me, Pet." His lips graze the shell of my ear, his warm breath claiming my neck, sending a sheet of goosebumps across my skin. But his mouth doesn't touch me. The lack of contact is torture, yet I know I'm already drowning in him.

Pet. Nobody has ever called me that. But something about that word and Zain's delivery stirs something deep in my belly, unleashing a confusing cocktail of arousal and a burning desire to belong to him, like some form of hypnosis.

I continue to rub myself furiously, holding onto the mirror in a futile attempt of stability before my legs give way, but Zain anchors me, his arm tight across my chest, clutching my shoulder in a death-like grip. His arousal, thick and hard, digs into my spine. I close my eyes again, arching into him, aching to feel something deeper. Two fingers plunge inside me, making my breath hitch and my heartbeat faster.

"Who do you belong to?"

"You. I belong to you," I breathe, my clit throbbing beneath my fingers. I know this is a game, but I entertain it.

"Good girl." Zain removes his fingers, brings them to his mouth and sucks them, watching me with hooded eyes as he savours the taste. Air leaves my lungs in violent bursts when he plunges them inside again, harder and deeper than the first time. "Come for me."

On command, my pussy clenches around his fingers, pleasure and release ripping through me as I tip over the edge, riding his fingers and mine over the waves of my orgasm as I shake against him. My vision is blurry, head light, my mind hazy, detached from my body. I'm whole, but I'm not. And when everything stills, I'm curled on the floor, a towel draped around me, my head resting on a lap clad in black denim, tattooed hands lightly stroking my hair and the scent of fire, water, and something else.

Redemption.

10

ZAIN

Millie sits on the couch, legs tucked underneath her, a glass of coconut water in her hand—which she winces at every time she takes a sip. She's wearing one of my flannel shirts from the '90s and thumbing through a book on Greek Mythology, and I have to say, that lumberjack aesthetic she's got going on is doing ungodly things to me.

"Hades and Persephone," I say, peering above the page she's stopped to read. "Interesting choice."

She takes a sip of her drink, grimaces, then sets it down on the side table. "I used to love learning about this stuff."

"What happened?" I wonder if she's ever read about me. Then again, I was never one of the important ones.

"I don't know. I lost interest, I guess." She runs a finger along the page like it has the answers she seeks. "Reality is miserable enough; we don't need to be reminded of it in fiction."

"What makes you think it's fiction?"

"Do you believe everything you read?" she asks.

"No, but we can still learn from things that aren't in our version of reality. Take Persephone, for instance. Mythology paints her like some victim," I say. "Open your mind to the possibility that she wasn't. That it was her fate to journey into the underworld."

"Absolutely. Nothing says meant-to-be like kidnapping and coercion." She slams the book closed and lays it in front of her.

"Your sarcasm exceeds you, Papillon," I say through gritted teeth.

She flashes a saccharine-sweet smile. Cocky little thing.

"Persephone needed to face her shadows, come out of her comfort zone, embrace her darkness, and step into her power without her mother's influence. She needed to realise that she was her own person—the Queen of the Underworld at that—and not just her mother's daughter."

She pins me with those earthy brown eyes. Now I have her full attention.

"Perhaps Hades' methods were unnecessary. But you can't deny that the journey Persephone took was her destiny. Rejecting a victim mentality and moving beyond her power, embracing who she really was, made her a Queen," I say.

Her smile wanes. Judging by her lack of words, I think I may have struck a nerve or, at the very least, challenged her perspective.

"Anyway," I continue, "we can talk about it on the drive. We need to get ready for solstice."

"Bold of you to assume I was coming. Besides, I don't have any clean clothes."

"Actually, you do."

I get on my knees and slide a duffle bag from beside the couch—a result of my escapades from the early hours of this morning when I couldn't sleep through thoughts of wanting her.

"Dead body?" she deadpans, peering at the opening with one raised eyebrow.

"Just the hands, half a leg, and a couple of rogue toes. The torso wouldn't fit." I unzip the bag and open it out so that she can see inside. She immediately recognises the contents and dives towards it. I shuffle out of the way to make space for her on the floor, and she kneels beside me. God, she smells good. A cocktail of citrus and sage shampoo. Fresh. Inviting. And the best part is that underneath it all, I still manage to catch a hint of her natural sweetness.

Her hand dips into the bag and pulls out the white sundress I picked out for the solstice celebration. "How did you get this?"

"I went to your flat last night."

"You did what? Are you out of your mind?"

"Relax. Nobody was home."

"I know that. I live on my own." Her cheeks glow red as she rifles through her belongings, then stops abruptly. "Wait, how the hell do you know where I live?"

"Your I.D."

"You *stole* my I.D. and *broke into* my house?" She's livid, and rightly so. It sounds worse when it's said out loud.

"Technically, I didn't break in. I had a key." In my defence, smashing a window at 2am wasn't an option, and I couldn't leave that damn note lying around.

"Fucking hell, Zain." She tenses, frozen for a moment when she sees the envelope with the words *Mum and Dad* scrawled across the front. Slowly, she reaches out and turns it over, her face visibly relaxing, an audible breath leaving her mouth when she sees that it's still sealed. "Do you have a lighter?"

I pull one from my back pocket and hand it to her. Then she gets up, takes the envelope to the kitchen and sets it alight in the sink, watching it burn to cinders.

I don't know what's written in there, and I don't need to. Yesterday is gone. Today, she'll have another chance.

11

MILLIE

I don't know where we're going. But all I know is that to-day, the desire to end my life doesn't feel as strong. Then again, it never does feel constant, and the continual ebbs and flows of a decision so... *final* means I would never take it light-ly. I've thought to no end of the irreparable damage I would cause—what it would do to my adoptive parents—knowing that they couldn't save me. Knowing that, unlike my blood mum, they actually wanted me. And they've tried to help; they really have. All that money wasted on therapy, hobbies long forgotten, holidays, gym memberships. But a soul as bitter and broken as mine is easier to give up than fight to save.

Zain's black Ford Capri is like something from the '80s, fully equipped with a tape deck and scratchy seats, and I'm doubtful that this vintage heap of junk will make the journey. There's no escape. And I fear these next two hours in confinement are going to be make or break when it comes to whatever this is between us. Despite the fact that I've spent a good chunk of time over the last twenty-four hours completely nude in Zain's presence,

I now feel more naked than ever. Vulnerability has never suited me, yet here we are.

Maybe I've been too quick to trust him, too impulsive to jump into a car and embark on a road trip with someone I've just met. Maybe I shouldn't have given him my body so easily, but this morning with Zain has redefined me, stripped away everything I thought I was. It's almost like I'm starting to feel human emotions again. These unfamiliar feelings of stepping into the unknown are a novelty, but they're a welcome one.

"Choose something you like." Zain's voice cuts through the silence. He leans over me and clicks open the glove compartment. Half a stack of cassette tapes falls onto my lap, the other half on the floor.

"You really should think about getting an MP3 player in here," I say, bending to pick them up.

"I think I'll stick to what I know, thanks. I've never been good with technology," he says.

"Okay, Grandpa."

I stack the tiny plastic boxes and study their covers. Deftones, Pixies, Kate Bush, The Cure...

I rearrange them as best I can, discarding the ones I haven't heard of, and I push The Smashing Pumpkins' aptly titled 1995 album Mellon Collie and the Infinite Sadness into the tape deck.

"Ah, Billy Corgan, the perfect driving companion. I'm impressed." He meets my gaze, smiles, then turns back towards the open road. Something about earning his praise makes my chest swell, and a warmth that's slowly becoming familiar gathers between my thighs.

I pull down the sun shade as She peaks in the sky. The roads are open, quiet, free from traffic, and the music soothes me from the inside out. And in the moments when Zain is focused on the drive, my eyes are free to linger on his handsome face. The sharp, the smooth, the light, the shadows. Those full, pillowy lips and the soft waves that fall around his face offsetting the sharpness of his jaw and the stark hollow of his cheekbones. The longer I look at him, the more I have to ask myself, is he real? How unfair that in a world of such ugliness, something so beautiful, so perfect, could exist?

"What are you thinking about?" he asks, rousing me from my musings.

"Nothing." *Everything*.

Despite my earlier reservations, the heap of metal surprisingly gets us there in one piece. We pull up next to a well-worn white camper van in a large, pebbled car park outside a thatched cottage with a sage green door surrounded by colourful flower beds, and the sign outside leads me to believe that it's a bed and breakfast.

"Gang's all here," he says, and I assume he's referring to whoever that camper van belongs to. My stomach twists. I'm not the biggest fan of meeting new people. Mostly because, at some point or another, I make a complete dick of myself. "Are you ready?"

No.

I fake a casual "yes" and unclick my seatbelt, even though I know I'm a terrible liar. Inked fingers thread through mine, and I know he can see right through me when he lays them in my lap, the white fabric of my dress shifting slightly upwards to expose more of my thigh.

"Look at me," he says.

Those otherworldly blue eyes sear through mine while my heart threatens to burst through my ribcage, pounding at such a speed that it makes me dizzy. To think that somebody I barely know can make me feel so much in such a short length of time is fucking with my head. Is the part of my mind that values my life trying to trick me into a false sense of security? That when the sun goes down, I won't be ready to go down with it?

Well, fuck you, brain. I'm going to enjoy this while it lasts. I know it's only temporary.

Zain's gaze cuts to the rear window, and my head turns. A stylish older lady with a bubblegum pink pixie haircut and an even brighter shade of lipstick stands in the doorway of the cottage. She's dressed in a floral housecoat, pink crocs, and a warm, radiant smile. She waves, and Zain waves back.

"That's Sylvie. She lets us use the car park twice a year for the festival." He turns to me and quirks a brow. "On the condition that she gets to feed us first."

"That's really sweet," I say, admiring the way his eyes light up when he talks about her. Maybe meeting her won't be so bad. He rounds the car and opens the trunk. "How long have you been coming here?"

"Forever. Sylvie's the grandmother I never had," he says. "She was my foster mum for a year when I was seventeen." He pauses, then shakes his head like he's shaking away a painful memory. "Anyway, we should get going."

"Don't get dressed on my account." Zain smirks, referring to Sylvie's dressing gown and crocs ensemble. I don't know how, but she manages to make it look relatively stylish.

She lovingly slaps his wrist, then opens her arms and pulls him in for a hug. It's beautiful to see and easy to forget that they aren't related by blood. Words in a foreign tongue tumble from her mouth. I try to decode the language, but it's muffled as she buries her head in the crook of Zain's neck.

When she finally lets him go, she meets my gaze. "Enchanté. I'm Sylvie."

"Millie," I say, holding out my hand. "It's lovely to meet you."

It's always awkward to be hugged by a stranger, but I don't have a choice when she takes my hand and pulls me towards her. She's warm, and she smells how I'd always imagined a grandmother to smell—powdery and floral, like Parma Violets. It's comforting.

"Lovely...just lovely," she says, holding me at arm's length. I mutter a quiet *thank you*, and even though Sylvie's compliment feels sincere, my gratitude doesn't. I'm not used to people being so openly complimentary to me, and I'm not sure it's something I could ever get used to. "Tres belle, no?" she says, turning her attention towards Zain with a wink.

"Ah, oui," he says, "mais on est seulement amis."

Amis. Friends. I wonder how many of his friends he's had his fingers in. The fact that he can openly diss me in another language and think I don't know what he's saying is insulting.

"Bullshit, darling." Sylvie turns to face me. Nevertheless, I appreciate her vote of confidence. "Come in, come in," she says, ushering us inside.

Despite the modest exterior, the open plan living area is sizeable, with wooden beams on the ceiling, and a large, open fireplace. On the far-right wall, there's a built-in bookcase. Mismatched sofas—one brown leather, the other navy-blue fabric, covered with patterned blankets and cushions in clashing shades of orange, yellow, green and grey—face a small round coffee table in the centre of the room. There are fresh flowers on every surface, and paintings of the countryside adorn the walls.

The decor looks as though everything has been carefully curated and collected over decades. Every object is unique and interesting, and no two are the same, but somehow it works. It's homely, and inviting, and I'm sure if the walls could talk, they'd have some stories to tell.

"Have a seat," Sylvie says.

I perch on the blue sofa while Zain peers his head around a small partition wall into the kitchen opposite. Without him, anxiety creeps into my stomach, and I feel a sudden vulnerability.

Then I hear a squeal. And in my next breath, a slight woman with wavy blonde hair throws her arms around Zain's neck.

Nausea smacks me right in the gut. I try to breathe it away, but it's pointless. I don't want to stare, but I can't help noticing the way Zain's large hands encircle her tiny waist. Or the way they fit together. It has me wondering how I fit into all of this. In such a short space of time I've never felt so unwelcome. So...forgotten. Why did he bring me here? It's almost better for me to have never known of his existence.

It's not like I ever belonged here, anyway.

I don't get attached to things easily, I never have. But when Zain pulls away and meets my gaze, relief washes over me, and my lungs compress.

"Millie, this is Jasmine," he says.

I don't miss the way her thrilled expression dampens before she schools herself into neutral, her pale green gaze meeting mine and offering what I fear is a less-than-genuine smile—and one purely for Zain's benefit. Perhaps I'm being paranoid, but it's far too early to know if she can be trusted, and I would never willingly play into my vulnerabilities like that. I know I have my own insecurities that stem from adolescence when it comes to pretty girls, so I straighten up, smile, and remind myself not to be so judgemental. Just because she looks like a Hollister model, it doesn't mean she's going to be like the rest of the cunts I knew in High School.

"Nice to meet you." I rise and try to smile as much as the anxiety will allow. But she's effortlessly beautiful in the way that makes others feel inferior. Namely, me.

"It's so lovely to meet you," she says, pulling me into a hug. She's surprisingly strong. I hug her back, mostly to please Zain, but it's not the worst thing in the world. She's warm, like Sylvie. Like Zain. And her smell—a soft, powdery scent, reminds me of wildflowers.

"Jas and I were in foster care together," Zain says.

"Oh." There is so much I don't know about him. So much I want to know, and I don't have a clue how to ask. What happened to his family? Why didn't anybody want to keep him? And was he fortunate to be taken in by two wonderful, loving people like I was?

I know it's a sensitive subject. That I'm one of the lucky ones. All my life, I've been told by strangers just how *lucky* I am that I was still a newborn when my mother decided to leave me. Everybody knows that the older the child, the less chance they have of finding a forever home.

"So, you're like brother and sister," I say.

Jasmine's scowl doesn't go undetected before it swiftly resets to neutral. But Zain laughs awkwardly. "I guess you could say that," he says. "Sylvie had all four of us here at once."

"Four?"

"Me, Jas, and her brothers, Josh and Jesse. Where are they, anyway?" he says, turning his attention back to her.

Jasmine cocks her head towards the kitchen. "Out back."

"Come on." He takes my hand and leads me through the kitchen to a set of French doors. Outside, two teenage boys with sweat-soaked golden hair kick a ball around, weaving the ball in between and around each other. They're too involved in the game to notice us, but when Zain shouts out, "Oi oi, lads," two identical faces with pale green eyes and a smile to rival their sisters' light up at the realisation of his presence.

One hour later, we're acquainted. And in that time, I learn a brief summary of how they came to know each other. Jasmine was taken into care when she was five years old. Her brothers, as soon as they were born, followed. Sylvie didn't acquire them until Jesse and Josh were ten, Jasmine thirteen. And shortly after, Zain—aged seventeen—ran away from his care home. Sylvie took him in, too. None of them elaborate on the details, but I don't push. I appreciate that they confide that much in me.

Zain's playful side shines through with every anecdote he recounts from adolescence. His fingertips graze my thigh when he speaks like it's nothing at all, while I find it increasingly harder to focus on the conversation when heat is rapidly spreading through my chest and between my legs, but I manage to react in all the right parts of the story. Mostly.

Jasmine excuses herself to grab a drink and doesn't return. I feel guilty for thinking it, but I'm relieved. Perhaps I'm reading too much into it, but suspicion niggles at the back of my mind, and I can't help but sense my presence is linked to her departure.

"Boys, come and help me in the kitchen," Sylvie says a moment later. I rise to help, as I've been raised to, but she halts me. "Not you, my dear. You're our guest."

"Come on," Zain says. "I'll show you the garden."

12

ZAIN

I light up a cigarette and offer it to Millie, but she declines. I don't want it either, but I take a drag anyway. She hasn't looked at me, let alone said a word, since we got outside.

I watch her from afar—like I always have—as she wanders around the garden aimlessly, stopping when something interesting catches her eye. A flower. A bee. A ceramic pot, edges shattered and misshapen, an effect of years of serving its purpose. She eventually settles by the wooden fence that overlooks the landscape surrounding Stonehenge. But there isn't a whole lot to see except acres of green.

I can't read her mind, but her energy is off, and it's killing me. Maybe I misread her. Maybe she's not ready yet. It's a big thing to expect someone you've just met to come and meet your family, and the last thing I want is to scare her away. I've been patient. Spent too much time and energy and planning to let her go because of one silly mistake. I never should have brought her here.

"I don't think that Jasmine girl likes me much," she says, finally breaking the silence.

I stub out the cigarette on the flower pot and flick it over the fence. Then I join her.

"Of course, she doesn't." My fingertips lift her chin to meet my gaze. "You're mine." She looks at me, wide-eyed, lips slightly parted, and I don't know if it's the effect of our proximity, my brutal honesty, or both. "Jasmine is..."

She breaks free from my grasp and stops to pick at a climbing clematis on the fence, the same colour as Sylvie's signature pink lipstick. "You don't owe me any kind of explanation. I know girls like Jasmine. And I know boys like you."

"What is it about boys like me?" I step closer, pinning her against the fence, boxing her in so she has no means to escape. Her breath quickens. The darkness clouding her energy lifts ever so slightly. She's staring at my mouth, and suddenly, that sadness turns to something else.

Hunger.

"Because I'd be happy to show you how I am *nothing* like anyone you've ever met," I growl. "If you think this morning was enough, you're mistaken. This morning was only the beginning. A fucking amuse bouche, Millie. Don't think for one second that I won't fuck the devil out of you. Because I sure as hell am willing to try."

She drags her bottom lip through her teeth, leaving my mind to race to the image of her on her knees, my cock cushioned inside that beautiful mouth. Trying to read her mind is futile, but I'm hoping that I haven't just hit the proverbial nail in the coffin.

Millie opens that sweet, heavenly, heart-shaped mouth to speak, but the moment ends when Sylvie's voice cuts through the silence. "Dinner's ready, darlings," she calls from the doorway.

Without hesitation, Millie brushes past me and walks towards the house.

Man, patience really is a virtue.

13

MILLIE

I manage to stay incognito during our meal, keeping my head down, minding my business, and reacting accordingly at the right moments. A smile here and there, a laugh, a sigh. The one time I dare to look up, those ocean-blue eyes entrap me. I don't know how long he's been staring, but the way Zain suggestively licks his fingers while pinning me with his gaze tells me it's been a while, and he's been waiting for the perfect opportunity to toy with me.

My stomach is aching from a lack of stimulation. And the worst part of this is that I'm feeling something that isn't my default of existential dread and despair. I can't remember the last time I masturbated, but since we met, it's all I think about. For so long, I've felt nothing, but being with Zain both excites and scares the ever-loving shit out of me. And I'm aware that I'm overthinking everything, that I should just go with it, reject my thoughts and return to the present.

"That was delicious, Sylvie. Thank you so much," I say, swiping a napkin across my mouth.

"You're welcome, my dear."

I rise to clear the plates, but Sylvie stops me.

"Darling, you're my guest. Let the boys do it," she says, cocking her head towards Josh, Jesse, and Zain.

"It's the least I can do, really," I say, offering her the only genuine smile I've had since I've been here. She returns the gesture and gracefully surrenders her plate.

"I'll give you a hand," Zain says, rising to collect the rest of the dinnerware.

Only bad things can come from being left alone with him, and we still have at least another sixteen hours or so on this trip, not including the journey home. But I reluctantly follow him into the kitchen. While he washes up, I dry, finding homes for everything and quietly obsessing over our proximity.

"Where does this go?" I ask, holding up a salad bowl.

"Right there." He cocks his head towards a shelf above him. With his hands immersed in water, I have no choice but to infiltrate his personal space. I reach up and place it on the shelf, then quickly retreat.

After a minute or so, his voice cuts through the silence. "Have I scared you or something?"

"What makes you think that?"

"Because you won't come near me."

The glass I've been drying for the past thirty seconds starts to squeak. "This entire situation is confusing, that's all. *You're* confusing."

"Why?"

"Because you think you know everything, and you don't. You don't know anything about me, Zain. And I have no idea what I'm doing here, but I'm done playing this game."

He turns to face me, pinning me with his gaze. "You think I've brought you here because it amuses me? Ah, sweet Millie...you couldn't be more wrong. I don't know what's given you the impression that I'm playing a game, but that's really not something I'm interested in." When he steps closer, I step back. "I don't pretend to know anything about you, but I know more than you think. I'll bet no one has ever bothered or taken the time to get to know the real you. Maybe it's because you won't let them. And I think you're scared of letting people in, of letting them see the real you. Fucked-up parts and all. Because then it might just be them who are scared. Because you think, for some messed-up reason, that you're unlovable or don't deserve to be happy. If you hide away your demons, if you convince yourself that you were never wanted, it's easier on your conscience when you decide to hurt the ones who actually want you here.

"And you're right, I don't know you, but I've observed you. I've wanted you, every shred of your being—your beauty, your light, your scars, your dark. I've wanted so badly to find out what makes you tick. To hurt you, to fuck you, to heal you. To be so deep inside you that you forget who you are, to make you feel like you never, ever want to leave this place..."

Well, fuck. That was a wake-up call. Before my mouth has a chance to catch up with the chaos running through my mind, the glass slips from my hands, crashing to the floor.

Instinctively, I gravitate towards it, careful that my bare knees don't touch the ground as I lay shards in my palm. Zain dries his hands and does the same.

"Millie, you're bleeding," he says, taking my hand to inspect the wound. The way the sticky red liquid constantly pours from the pad of my index finger makes me lightheaded. The sight of blood hits different when it isn't self-inflicted.

"I'm fine. It doesn't hurt," I say. I'm pretty sure my ego is the most fragile thing in this room right now.

"I don't think there's any fragments in there," he says, squeezing the flesh.

More blood pours from the wound, then he wraps his mouth around my finger and sucks. Hard. At first, it takes me by surprise, but then I let him.

And I like it.

His cheeks hollow out, accentuating those glorious cheekbones, and those eyes...God, those eyes. Dark and unpredictable like a summer storm, making me dizzy with want, and I just know he's really fucking enjoying himself. And when the flow eases, I smear the blood along his bottom lip like war paint. Marking my territory. All these fucked-up parts of me wish he would drain every ounce from my body. What a magical way to die.

"Mmm." His full lips quirk into a smile. "I can't help myself when you taste so good."

The door swings open, and I pull my hand away when I see Jasmine walk in. I feel oddly embarrassed, like we've just been caught doing something we shouldn't.

"Everything okay in here?" she asks. By the look on her face, she knows she's interrupted something.

"Fine," Zain says.

"I smashed a glass," I say.

"Oh. Do you need a hand?" she asks.

"We got it," he says.

"Okay. We're going in ten minutes," she says, lingering for a moment before leaving the same way she came in.

Zain proceeds to bend down, eyes on me as he picks up shard after shard, while all I can think about is how good he looks on his knees.

14

MILLIE

I'm not cut out for this kind of exercise.

After barely eating the last couple of days, extreme hunger has finally caught up with me, and now it's starting to materialise. My head is light, my legs like jelly, and the only thing I really want to do right now is curl up on the grass and go to sleep. Not to mention the fact that the air is so humid that it's almost unbreathable. But the view could be worse. Zain is dressed in black skinny jeans and a t-shirt with some obscure band I've never heard of, and I can't stop staring at him. At least his presence is giving me the momentum to carry on.

Periodically, he'll turn around to check in, and every time he does, it catches me off guard, and I have to pretend that I haven't just been freely ogling to my heart's content.

Once we reach the outskirts of the stone circle, he stops and waits for me, letting the others take the lead while my feet catch up with his, my heart throbbing from exertion.

"Here we are," he says, his voice steady and rhythmic as always, his appearance so perfectly untouched that nobody would know that he's been hiking across farmland for the best part of an hour.

Now that it's evening, the thirty-degree heat from the day has eased off to a reasonable twenty. But I'm still struggling with the humidity.

I didn't think this world could be any more disappointing, but I am completely and utterly underwhelmed at the sight of Stonehenge.

"It's a bit...small," I deadpan.

"That's what she said." He laughs, sweat dripping from his hairline, and I try to shy away from thoughts of licking it away. "Come on, size isn't everything."

"That's what *he* said."

"Touchez, Papillon."

He might not realise it, but Zain is far more impressive than any wonder of the world. He puts his arm around me, and we start to walk again, side by side. I think about this morning. To those hands on me. In me. Bonfire smoke fills my lungs, and noise pollutes the air. The sound of percussion, of drums and wind instruments, and the distinct sound of the wilderness.

"Some people say that Stonehenge is a giant fertility symbol," Zain says. "You can't see it from this angle, but from an aerial view, it looks like a female sexual organ."

"It looks like a bunch of rocks to me."

"There's symbolism in everything, Millie. You just have to find what something means to you. There's no right or wrong.

"Some people say it has strong connections to Mother Earth, that the central area represents the opening of which she gave birth to plants and animals. It's a place of life and birth, a place that looks to the future. Rebirth, creation, and regeneration.

Others say that the stones were placed in such a way that cast phallic shadows."

"Man, what a way to celebrate the patriarchy," I say dryly.

"I'll show you my favourite one later."

"You have a dick shadow preference?"

"Doesn't everyone?" Zain says, squeezing my shoulder in a way that makes my body lean into his.

We sit on blankets on the ground beside one of the monoliths. One of the twins sparks a joint and offers it to me, but I don't take it. The other one hands me a paper cup filled with honey-coloured liquid.

"What is this?" I ask.

"Mead," he says proudly. "I made it myself."

I take the cup out of politeness, but I don't intend on drinking the whole thing. I haven't consumed any alcohol or drugs since last night, and I'm not sure I want to.

"If and when I plan on fucking you, Papillon...I need you to be in the right headspace. Sober. Understand that I will ruin you for anyone else."

Zain's words from last night have clearly had an effect.

As long as nobody offers to top up my drink, I'll be okay.

I take a sip. It's smooth and a little dry, but I enjoy the taste. Not that I'm a mead connoisseur by any measure. And when the sandwiches are passed around, I make sure I fill up on those instead.

By late afternoon, the entire place is filled to the brim with people, all in varying stages of sobriety. Music plays, the tone is mellow, and our bellies content. And although Stonehenge is nothing special to look at, the energy it exudes is strangely magical.

"Come on," Zain says, taking my hand again.

"Where are we going?" I ask.

"You'll see."

The inner circles have a lot more foot traffic than I'm comfortable with, but Zain doesn't let go of my hand. I'm not used to being around so many people. I was home-schooled for the final years of my academic life. I didn't go to college or university and never go to parties. The only friends I have are the online ones who enable my suicidality.

Zain leads the way through clusters of crowds towards a pair of capped rock pillars that are roughly twice his size, and it's only now that I'm standing directly underneath it that I can marvel at its height. I'm too busy admiring the structure to notice him prising the cup from my hands and pouring the liquid onto the floor until it's too late.

"I was drinking that!" I say.

"No, you weren't."

I glower, but I can't keep up the façade for long, especially when I'm faced with his shit-eating grin, which infuriates me even more.

"This is what I wanted to show you," he says, pausing to make sure I'm listening. "The two vertical stones symbolise the mother and father. The dark, mysterious, feminine yin, and the light, extrovert, masculine yang. See up there." He gestures towards the rock above our heads. "That's where they unite. The reason we celebrate summer solstice is to celebrate the sun's closest approach to Earth. The rise of the mid-summer sun fits with the notion of the Earth Mother and the Sun Father. In mid-winter, they are the furthest apart, and in mid-summer, they reunite, as nature intended." He turns to the stone on our right. "You see how this one is smooth, and the other is rough?"

"If I wanted a geography lesson, I would have stayed in school," I say in a last-ditch attempt to save face. But he disregards my comment and continues. No matter how hard I try, I can't seem to get under his skin the way he has mine.

"Technically, the stones are off limits to wandering hands, but there aren't any cameras here." His gaze darkens, and heat creeps up my neck. "Think of all the things I could do to you right in front of these people." His fingers skirt the hem of my dress, his mouth grazing the shell of my ear. "I bet you'd like that, wouldn't you? I could ruin that greedy little cunt in the middle of this crowd, and nobody would ever know."

Oh fuck.

"Now, are you going to listen? Or shall I make you lean against this rock with your ass in the air and spank you until you can't sit down?"

The second one sounds more appealing, if I'm honest. But I don't doubt that he'll follow through on that. "I'll listen."

"Good girl."

The next few minutes are a blur. I try to pay attention, but all I can think about is getting railed against these rocks. It amazes me how his personality can switch almost instantly. It's like he's two different people. Yin and yang.

My ears zero in on a small group of people playing various percussion instruments before tuning back into my conversation with Zain, but it seems I've missed the whole thing. "I need to find a bathroom," he says. "See you back at camp?" He doesn't seem to notice that I haven't been listening this entire time.

"Sure." I turn and head towards the direction of the group, away from the music, disappointed that I didn't choose the latter option, after all.

"Oh, Millie?" I spin back around to face Zain. He crooks his finger into a come hither movement. I start towards him, and he meets me halfway. "You forgot to give me your panties."

"Excuse me?"

"You want me to say it louder?"

"No," I say, in hushed tones. He really is the most unpredictable person I've ever met.

"Don't you know it's disrespectful to be lost in your thoughts when I'm talking to you, Pet? I want you to be present with me at all times, understand?" I'm lost for words, my brain completely devoid of a single coherent thought. "Panties. Now."

"You want me to take them off...here?"

He nods. "Right in this spot."

"But what if someone sees?"

"It's not illegal to go commando, Papillon."

I'm more embarrassed about the subtle act of pulling them down and giving them away, but I'll admit that the idea of Zain carrying around my soaked underwear is a massive turn-on. I glance around, trying not to make it glaringly obvious to any onlookers, and I pull down the lace fabric. Once they're over my thighs, I let them drop past my knees to my ankles. Then I quickly bend down, as if to tie my shoelace, and step out of them. Zain is smirking the entire time, and when I ball them up and hand them over, I try my best to scowl.

"Mm, already so wet." He handles the fabric carefully, but he's anything but subtle. "You'll get these back once you learn how to behave," he says, pocketing them. "Or you won't." He kisses me, catching me off guard. And it starts and ends so fast that I have to question whether it happened at all. "I'll see you soon."

Dear God, I'm going to hell.

15

ZAIN

Holy fuck, I'm going to hell. At least that's where I *would* be going if I was mortal.

I had to make any excuse to get away from Millie before my dick burst through the seam of my jeans. In hindsight, I could have chosen a better place than a Portaloo to hide. Not even the foul stench of piss and shit can distract me from wanting to rub myself to the memory of the sweet, pale pink glow of her cheeks and the way those big brown eyes shone like beacons when I praised her.

What a fucking good girl.

I take her panties from my pocket and bring them to my nose, inhaling her scent so deep that the sweetness fills my lungs and makes my head rush, emptying my mind of anything but her. I could get high on her smell alone, but I need something stronger. Something painful. Violent. I need to forget that I won't be here tomorrow.

I pull down my zipper, take out my dick, and light a cigarette. I'm pretty sure you're not supposed to smoke in these chemical-laden cubicles, but I need something to take the edge off.

Precum beads around the tip. I lace it with spit and rub her panties along my length, letting my mind wander to this morning. The taste of her skin. Her gasps, her moans. The way that tight little cunt gripped my fingers like a lifeline as I buried them inside her.

"Who do you belong to?"

"You. I belong to you."

Fuck. If only I could take my little souvenir to Summerland.

Maybe I don't deserve her, but either way, she's unravelling every part of me I've learned to control. All the ugliness and darkness. The shadows, the morbid, the melancholy. And I don't care. I need this to be enough for her before I give in to the control once and for all. I never plan to be in my bodies for long, but this feels like it could be the right fit for a little while longer. Though I know when the time comes, I need to be prepared to let it go.

I edge myself, easing off with lazy strokes when it gets too much. But I won't let myself cum. I tell myself it's because my seed deserves better than to swim around in the nuclear blue chemicals of a toilet bowl. Which is true, but it's also not the whole reason. Since last night especially, I've been aching to be inside that sweet cunt. I need to be buried inside of her. I need to be so deep that our souls are touching. The next time I'm close to orgasm, I press the cigarette to my forearm and hold it there.

Fuck. It stings like hell. But I welcome the pain. I need it. I wait until it subsides, when all that remains is a slow-burning and intense euphoria.

I toss the rest of the cigarette into the toilet and tuck myself away, taking a moment to compose myself. Now the smoke has cleared, I can't stay in this putrid hotbox any longer. My dick will have to get over himself in the great outdoors.

As soon as the plastic door swings open, I'm caught off guard. Jasmine.

Did she know I was here?

I dig my hands into my pockets and attempt to rearrange myself, but it's too late; she's already noticed the swell in my jeans.

"Oh. I was wondering when you'd make an appearance," she says, smirking. I'm not sure if she's speaking to me or my dick, but the shit-eating grin on her face suggests the latter. "Little Miss Sunshine not living up to your expectations?"

I choose not to answer; I know she's not expecting one. Her pupils constrict in slow motion every time she blinks, her skin tinged with grey, the youth sucked from her face. The dried-out look of someone who's ingested too much alcohol. I love Jasmine, but she's not a good drunk. She's fun for a while, but if she doesn't have her way, she gets aggressive. The realities of being friends with a dryad. Chaotic little tree bastards. Luckily, my dick and I know that he can stay firmly in my pants when I'm around her because we both know that she isn't Millie.

"Come on, Zain. Be real. You know she's not going to give you what you need. Nobody ever does." She backs me up against the plastic box, pressing her body into me as she stands on her tiptoes. Her mouth grazes the shell of my ear, sending a shiver down my spine, and not a good one. "You think anyone can fuck you like I can?" She presses her fingertips into my forearm, the afterburn of the cigarette intensifying as her fingers dig into my skin. I wince, but she's trying so hard to hold herself upright that I know the pain on my face won't register.

I don't know how much she's had to drink since I've been gone, but I know Jesse's mead is lethal. One cup is fine, but any more, and you're a goner. It's one of the reasons I hardly touch the stuff. I don't like the person Zain becomes when he drinks; it must be something to do with the composition of his DNA. Luckily, *I* have some semblance of self-control.

Jasmine is a feisty, fragile thing. She's like a fucking bomb that will destroy everything if she doesn't get her own way, and I can't risk anything right now, not when I have Millie where I want her. Not when I'm so damn close. But when Jasmine's tongue runs along my neck, and a hand that isn't mine is placed firmly on my dick, it's the final straw. "Jasmine, stop."

"You know you don't mean that."

"I'm deadly fucking serious. Get your hand off my dick."

"You want me to beg, is that it?"

I shove her hand away. "This isn't a game, Jas. We're not together. We never were. So, get it out of your head that we ever will be."

She backs up, taking a moment to compose herself. "It's *her*, isn't it?" Black holes pool the green of her eyes. Her mood turns sombre. Her tone poisonous. "You haven't told her yet, have you?"

"Told me what?"

Fuck. My stomach does a backflip. I spin around.

Millie stands there, taking in the scene. A mixture of hurt and rage in equal measure etched across her beautiful face.

"You know what? Forget it. I've seen enough." She turns and walks away before I have the chance to explain.

How much did she hear? I know she deserves to know the truth, but I have no reason to feel guilty, so why do I feel like I've done something wrong?

I go after Millie. After the shit Jasmine has pulled, I couldn't give a fuck if she spends the rest of the night fucking every stranger in this place until she passes out. She can take care of herself. It's Millie I have to worry about.

16

MILLIE

"Millie, wait." Zain's voice cuts through my periphery, but it's all I can do to keep walking without losing my shit.

Granted, I knew I couldn't trust them. I should have minded my business, but on the way back to camp, I saw something I've never seen before. Something I never knew existed in this part of the country. A blue butterfly.

I took it as a sign and followed it, and it led me straight to Zain and Jasmine's little tryst. I should have known this was too good to be true.

Fuck them. I don't know what's worse; the fact that she had her hand on his dick, that he let her, or that I even entertained the thought of coming here in the first place. I've never had real friends; why should any of that change now? And why should it matter? I'll be gone soon enough.

"Do you have any mead left?" I ask one of the twins. My voice is shaking with anger, but I try to keep it level.

Josh hands me the half-empty Kilner bottle. I don't even bother to pour it into a glass—I'm taking it with me. The first sip takes the edge off instantly, but when I see Zain approach, hurt and anger rips my stomach to shreds.

"Millie, can we talk?" he asks.

"No, I'm good, thanks." I'm proud of myself for not raising my voice. For keeping calm and refusing to break. I keep my gaze trained on the ground. I know if I look into those eyes, I'll weaken.

"Millie." This time, his voice is stern. Authoritative. But I don't put down my proverbial guns. A moment passes, then I'm held against my will by his words. "Millie, please."

This is a new one; I've never been begged before. But it's something I could get used to.

I take another sip. But I still don't look at him. I'm torn. Part of me wants to hear him out, and the other part wants to run away and never look back. I choose the latter, taking the bottle with me. I don't know where I'm headed, but all I know is that I need to get the fuck away from here.

I head towards the centre of the stone circle, amidst all the chaos, in the hopes that I can lose Zain in here. It's so noisy I can barely hear myself think, but I can still hear the constant call of my name.

Once I'm through the other side of the stone circle, in the open landscape, I take a breath and let my heart slow. Then I carry on walking. And my musings help me realise the reason I was wary of Jasmine from the start. She's an alpha. The past version of me before I discovered the real truth about my mother and became a shadow of my former self. Someone I'll never get back.

I was happy. Loved. Wanted.

I had a family.

When I approach a lone monolith in the clearing, I stop to catch my breath. I've walked enough for the lump in my throat to subside, but the anger remains. I turn around to see how far I've come. Everyone looks like ants. Everyone except Zain.

His eyes shine like glass in the sunlight, and I never fully understood the term butterflies until now. I wasn't expecting him to follow me here, and I'll admit, his powers of persuasion are impressive—I wish I had his resilience. But I don't know if his persistence makes me ready to forgive what I've just seen.

"Are you done running away from me?"

"I don't know. Are you done having someone else's hand on your dick?" Could I be any more pathetic? Twenty-four hours ago, I didn't even know he existed. I don't exactly have a reason to be jealous. I need to keep telling myself that he's not my property, but I can't help myself. I feel as though I've been lulled into a false sense of security, tricked into thinking he wanted this, wanted *me*.

"I guess I deserved that." He slinks right past me to the monolith, shrugs off of his backpack, opens it, and takes out a bottle of water. After unscrewing the cap, he offers me the first sip. I'm parched, but I don't want him to read anything into it. I'm not going to accept an olive branch that easily. "Drink some water, or you'll dehydrate. You're no good to anyone if you're passed out."

"Quit telling me what to do."

"Quit being so stubborn."

I roll my eyes and swipe the bottle from his hands, spilling the contents on the floor. The first sip tastes like heaven, and it takes everything I have to hold myself back from draining the entire thing.

I pass the bottle back. Seeing this man's thirst satiate with every gulp has me practically drooling, and I have to keep reminding myself that I'm supposed to be mad. But it makes me wonder if he knows exactly what he's doing.

"Why did you bring me here?" I ask.

"Why not?" He takes a seat on the grass by the monolith and pats the space beside him. "Come sit."

Since I have no way of getting out of here, I may as well listen to what he has to say. I perch next to him, leaning my back against the monolith, my legs tucked underneath me, my hands on my thighs.

"I should have told you about Jasmine. What happened back there...that was all her. We have history, but I don't see her like that. Not the way I see you." Inked hands graze the earth. Gently, he plucks a daisy from the grass and proceeds to trace the petals across the scar on my leg. "I like you, Millie. And the only hand I want on my cock"—he slides the daisy into my palm—"is yours."

The only thing that scares me more than living is that even when he's touching me indirectly, I can feel his energy—his light—so strongly. Is this what he means by being an empath? It seems like he's the only person in the world I feel connected to.

Zain picks another daisy. "Did you know the daisy is Freya's flower? She's the goddess of love, fertility, and motherhood. In Norse mythology, daisies were given as a gift to congratulate new mothers. In pagan times, daisy chains were thought to cast a protective circle."

Slowly, he traces the contours of my calf with the petals, moving higher up past my knee, then my thigh, until he reaches the hem of my dress. He slips it underneath, and the head disappears, leaving only the thin green stalk in my line of sight. My breath catches when he stops, part of me thinking that if I hold my breath long enough, he'll give me what I want.

"I want to fuck you in this dress," he says, and it comes out so calm and unexpected that I hardly believe it. He keeps his gaze trained on the daisy, on my thighs, and my awareness shifts towards the swelling in his jeans. Perhaps it's time I stop listening to these limiting beliefs—they've never served me well in the past.

"Then fuck me," I say.

"Not yet. You need to know the truth."

17

MILLIE

I've never known anxiety like this. I'm not sure what to expect, but the truth must be pretty groundbreaking if Zain has been putting off telling me this entire time.

"The night we met, I wasn't supposed to..." He pauses to collect his thoughts. "I was supposed to guide you on your way to the spirit world. But when I saw you, I wanted you, and I would have done anything to have you. I know it's wrong and so fucking selfish of me, but I had to *know* you.

"It didn't feel right that you were going to so easily—and don't get me wrong—bravely—leave this world of your own accord, but it seemed like such a waste. I've met people heading down the same path as you, and it was right for them—it was their destiny. But you, Millie? I know you have so much more to give. You deserve more than the cards you were dealt."

I have so many questions, but I can't find the words.

"Once a year, I die. Then six months later, I'm reborn." He pauses to gauge my reaction, but I'm pretty certain my mixed emotions are completely unreadable. "After solstice, when the sun splits the horizon, my soul leaves my body, and I reunite with my form in the underworld. I live there for six months, then when winter solstice comes around, I'm reborn back into my human body...this body...on Earth."

I try to catch a hint of a smirk, but his expression gives nothing away.

"I know this sounds utterly ridiculous, but it's the truth," he adds.

"You're fucking with me, right?"

"I wish I was." He looks at the floor and takes a deep breath, then his eyes find mine. And somehow, I know that this is real.

"You live in the underworld? Isn't that the same as hell?" Realisation dawns on me. Was my mother trying to warn me through her tarot cards?

"Not exactly. There are different realms in hell. The Underworld—or Summerland as we like to call it—is where I reside. It's the place I nurture and prepare lost souls."

"Who are you?" I ask.

"I'm a deity. Cernunnos is my immortal name."

It doesn't exactly roll off the tongue, but it's better than Satan or Lucifer.

"Do you look...like you?"

"Not exactly. When my soul is in the underworld, my physical appearance is altered. Facially, there are similarities. But my hair is longer, I'm broader, taller, hairier, hornier..."

"Hornier as in you have horns, or you're doubly insatiable?"

"A little of both," he says.

I smile. Though I'm still unsure how to take this new information, I'm willing to give him the benefit of the doubt. And if all this was purely a ruse to lift my mood, he's succeeded. "What I wouldn't give to see that," I say.

"I have some mythology books with illustrations of me in them, but they're not that accurate. There's not a lot about me in those books; I just get lumped together with Pan and the other horned gods."

"What do they say about you?"

"That I'm the god of the underworld, bringer of death. I'm lusty and fertile, a master of wild animals and the hunt."

"Does that make me a wild animal?" I ask.

"It makes you prey." His eyes narrow, sending a shot of adrenaline straight to my core. "Do you want to play a game?"

"What kind of game?" I don't know what the hell is going on, but I'm not ready for this to end. This entire experience has felt like a game. What harm will one more do?

"How much ground can you cover in three seconds?"

"Are you serious?"

"Do I look like I'm joking?" Suddenly, he looks more demon than human.

"Not enough," I reply in answer to his previous question.

"Then you'd better get running."

My heart is pounding. Fear and excitement wash over me.

"Three." He's looking at me with a hunger in his eyes that I can't place, but it's fuelling the heat between my legs. Humidity has hit his long dark hair, making him look completely wild. A fallen angel who has long since lost his wings. And I know if I don't move soon, he might just eat me alive.

"Two."

Fight-or-flight kicks in, and without another thought, I get up and run as fast as I can, in the opposite direction from the crowds into the vast, empty landscape.

"One."

I want him to chase me, to catch me. I know it's only a game, but I won't let him have me too easily. I glance behind, and that one moment of hesitation is all it takes before I'm caught in the clearing. Well, that didn't last long.

Zain catches me from behind, one arm around my waist, the other across my chest, anchoring me. I struggle, trying my best to free myself from his grasp, flailing and kicking my legs out behind me, but I'm too weak. Perhaps I don't want my freedom badly enough to fight for it.

"Feisty little thing, aren't you?" His lips brush the shell of my ear, sending shivers all the way down my spine. For a moment, he eases his grip on me. "This gets too much, call red. Got it?" I nod. "Words, girl. Use your words."

"Yes," I breathe. I am completely at his mercy.

"Good." He tightens his grip on me again, then throws me down. I land on my hands and knees. Lush grass cushions my fall, filling my head with its sweet, fresh scent. "Don't move until I tell you to." He toes his boot under the hem of my dress, inching it up over my ass and pussy, baring all for the entire world to see.

A cool breeze brushes across my bare flesh, making me squirm, adding to the ache. I'm not sure how much longer I can withstand a lack of stimulation, but I don't dare move. I clench my thighs together and count the seconds. A minute passes, and I'm left wondering if I've been abandoned. But then I hear his voice.

"What a pretty cunt," he muses. The cool, hard leather of his boot glides along my slit from front to back. "Already dripping for me." I revel in the contact. My breath hitches as I imagine him on his knees, his face buried between my thighs. But the fantasy is short-lived.

He paces around me, taking calculated steps before crouching in front of me. I want to crawl onto his boot and hump the leather like a fucking dog. Anything for a sliver of relief.

"You know what to do," he says. I don't. At least I don't think so. I know what I want to do, but there are sordid parts of my brain that I've never understood or considered *normal*. Parts of me that no one has ever understood, and I'm not willing to assume that we're on the same page. "Lick it off."

Heat floods between my thighs, like some kind of knee-jerk reaction. I've never done anything like this. I wouldn't even know where to start. But the idea of something so humiliating sparks something inside that both terrifies and excites me.

I inhale, filling my lungs with the scent of leather, and run my tongue along the glistening toe cap, licking the vamp, all the way up to the laces, and to the worn, weathered ankle. They taste like me, mixed with kicked-up dust and a distinct sweetness. Like bitterness and shame. I never knew that something so dirty and degrading could feel so exhilarating, yet here we are.

"That's enough now, Pet," he says. I stop mid-lick. "We can't have you peaking too soon." His fingers coax my chin to meet his lustful gaze. "If I didn't know any better, I'd say you were enjoying that," he smirks, his tone eager. Mocking. "Open your mouth."

I do as he says, lifting my head and opening wide to accept my reward. Just like a fucking dog. A perfect pool of saliva drips from his mouth into mine. He tastes sweet like honey, satiating like smoke. Heat rushes between my legs, my arousal intensifying.

"Good girl," he says.

This is torture. All I want is to feel the weight of his cock inside me. His heaviness, his fullness. And I know he wants it, too; the tent in his jeans doesn't lie.

"You're going to kill me," I moan.

"That's never been my intention." He stands, towering over me, and I can't help but revel in his arousal. I clench my thighs in desperation. If everything he's told me is true, then we don't have much time, and I fully intend to make the most of the time we do have.

Once again, he skulks around me, taking slow, measured steps in those black lace-up boots I've just had the pleasure of licking clean.

My peripheral gives nothing away, but I can feel him crouching down behind me. Stealthy fingers slip between my folds. I exhale, revelling in the relief. It's a small feat, but it's not nearly enough. I need more.

"Please," I say.

"You'll need to beg better than that, Papillon," he says eagerly as he palms my ass.

"Please." Crack. I gasp, shocked at the unexpected impact of his hand. "Fuck me." Crack. "Master." Crack. My breath hitches with every blow. I don't know what possessed me to address him so... formally, but it sounds like the right answer.

"Better." Zain's fingers plunge into me, a pathetic whimper escaping my mouth as my pussy clenches greedily around them. "Head on the ground," he says, spreading my knees apart as I bury my face in the earth.

My ears prick up at the sound of a zipper, leaving me wondering if his cock is already in his hand. I envision him stroking himself, getting off on getting me off. Arching my hips back into him, I ride his fingers while his thumb circles my clit. Pressure builds inside of me, an infusion of colour clouding my vision, my chest pounding, the sweet smell of grass filling my head as the world falls away.

"I'm going to come," I breathe.

When I think he's finally going to let me orgasm, he slows, withdrawing his fingers.

I gasp at the sudden lack of contact, my pussy throbbing from the void. Before my emotions have a chance to regulate, his fingers fill me again, splaying inside me, stretching me.

"Oh, God," I moan, cringing when I realise the irony of my words. "Please...please fuck me."

His fingers slow once more, and I'm left to wonder if I've made a momentous mistake.

"Well, since you asked so nicely..." Zain keeps his fingers stretched at my entrance as he eases himself in. I breathe through discomfort as he slowly, carefully fills me with the weight I've been craving. "God, you feel like heaven," he says, his breath ragged, voice heavy with lust. That sound alone could spark an orgasm in me.

He slams into me, punching air from my lungs with every thrust. Fire spreads beneath my skin, every part of me set ablaze for him as I dig my nails into the ground, like I'm trying to claw my way to the Earth's core.

"Good girl. You're taking me so well." Zain's hand slides to my clit, stroking me with teasing circles, his growing urgency making me jerk and groan unabashedly as his skin smacks against mine. "Come for me, angel."

My orgasm rips through me. Hard and violent and hurting—and it's all I've ever wanted. Vision hazy, head empty, heart open. I close my eyes.

"Fuck." He jerks, his cock pulsing inside me as he slowly withdraws. Hot cum spurts onto my skin, marking me, claiming me.

This is the most sated I've ever been. The most full. The most grateful to be alive—to experience something so close to death. And despite my scars, despite my dirty fingernails and grass-stained knees—I feel purified. Cleansed from the inside out, connected to every life force on this Earth; every grain of sand, every drop of water in the ocean.

Death is literally dripping down my thighs, and I never want to wash Him off.

18

ZAIN

"Does it hurt?" Millie asks, those earthy brown eyes full of naiveté and expectation.

My back rests against the monolith, legs outstretched. She's lying sideways on the grass with her head on my thighs. "When I rise from hell, or?" Now isn't the time to be joking, but I want to lighten the mood as much as I can before I leave. Maybe then she'll remember me fondly.

She catches me with a sardonic glare. "You know what I mean. Is it painful...when you die?" She swallows hard and looks away as if she doesn't really want to know the answer.

Suddenly I'm angry at myself. I had no right to do this to her. To add to the death and destruction she's already had to endure. If nothing else, I owe her my honesty.

"I wish I could say I fall into a deep sleep while my soul peacefully drifts over to the other side, but my physical body has to prepare itself first," I say.

Millie meets my gaze with intent—almost like she's trying to remember every minor detail of my face.

"At sunset, I start to weaken. My arms and legs fatigue, then my brain; I lose my eyesight, my hearing, and my speech slurs. My muscles start to ache, almost like a stretching sensation—sort of like growing pains. Over hours, it spreads, gradually getting worse until the pain is so debilitating, I can't move. Sylvie puts me in a therapeutic coma, hooks me up to a feeding tube, monitors me—she and her ancestors have taken care of me for generations. My soul leaves when my body is stable, and the next time I wake, I'm in Summerland."

"What do you do there, exactly?"

"You know I said my winter job is to guide the souls to the underworld? Well, my summer job is to prepare the old souls for rebirth."

"Like reincarnation?"

"Exactly."

She nods like she understands, but she's distant in her mind. "Can you die?"

"Technically, no. But I can be defeated, I guess. I can be imprisoned in my own body or in nature—the way the Greek God Atlas was. Or I can be chopped up and the pieces separated."

Clearly, she's horrified, so I brush over the subject. I don't want to freak her out. "There are lesser-known ways to kill a deity, and some have ways to die that are only specific to them."

Like falling in love with a mortal.

"Earlier at the cottage, when you said...that you've watched me...did you mean..."

"I was there the first time. When you were fifteen. I've always been there."

"Why did you let me live?"

"I...I don't know how to answer that."

"Try." Pleading eyes glaze over, hurt plastered over her face, and I know that she's thinking the worst—that she wasn't good

85

enough for me to take her. But that couldn't be further from the truth.

How do I tell her that she deserves better? That she deserves to achieve greatness, to have a chance at being the mother she never had—if that's something she would want. That she deserves to right all the wrongs that have plagued her for her entire life. That she deserves to have a fresh start after everything she's been through.

That she's far too good for me.

"It wasn't your time," I say quietly. If it's a cop-out answer, then so be it. At least I'm being honest.

She glides her fingers over the grass and plucks a daisy. "I don't believe you," she says, but her smile says otherwise.

"Well, that's rude." I lean towards her personal space, lowering my voice. "Perhaps I just wanted you for myself."

"I'm still not buying it," she says, grounding me in her gaze. Her energy tells me otherwise. I lean in, but she covers her mouth.

"I'm so dehydrated," she says, her voice muffled.

"I'm so past caring." I slide her hand away, her eyes closing when I plant a kiss on her forehead. "I'll be back."

"Where are you going?" She sits up when I start to move my legs, giving them a little shake to wake them up.

"To get you some water."

"But what if I get eaten by a wild animal?"

I laugh. "First of all, you're more likely to die of dehydration than any chance of that happening. And second, the only wild animal that's even allowed to *think* about eating you is me."

19

ZAIN

G olden hour sets in when I return, emitting soft yellow light over the landscape. Everything looks more gentle, more beautiful, right before the sun goes down. It's bittersweet because I know we don't have much time left. Within the next hour, I'll start to deteriorate.

Millie sleeps by the monolith, her body laid sideways on the grass, knees curled up into a foetal position, her head resting on one hand, the other outstretched with a chain full of daisies wrapped around her delicate fingers, as lengthened shadows cast across her still, sleeping body; one half bathed in light, the other in darkness. Yin and yang.

And it's only now that I have the chance to fully appreciate her beauty.

I'm careful not to disturb her, but when I crouch beside her, she stirs as if she can sense me. A sheen of sweat covers her skin, her breath ragged. But I can't tell if she's having a nightmare or dreaming.

Carefully, I prise the chain from her delicate grasp, tie the loose ends together and place it on top of her head like a crown. Of all the daisies blooming in this field, she picked the flawed ones. Violet-hued, closed ones, sparse ones. I smile. She's starting to see the beauty in imperfection, the light in the dark. In brokenness, ugliness, and scars.

I wish I could keep her.

My mind maps the scene. White canvas shoes cast aside on the grass, dusty with kicked-up soil. The way her small chest heaves with every breath, the way the sunlight kisses her shoulders. The sprinkle of dark hair on her forearms. Dirt under fingernails. The scent of earth and sex. Wild. Feral. Beautiful. My dick strains against my jeans, and suddenly it's not enough to simply observe. I need to be touching her.

I stroke the hair from her face. She stills, her mouth curling into a soft smile, the crease in her forehead slowly smoothing.

I lay behind her, propping myself on my elbow as I reach around to rest my hand on her thigh. Sighing, she burrows her body into mine, leaving no room in between as I cocoon myself around her and slide my hand between her legs.

I cup her, my palm laid flat against her, making her breath hitch. She raises her hips, parting her knees to accommodate me. Her soft, sweet cunt is already slick with arousal; it has me wondering if it's a dream that has her soaked or me. I bring my fingers to my mouth and suck her juices, savouring the taste of her, and slide my hand back between her legs. It might be due to the fact that I haven't eaten in hours, but she's the sweetest thing I've ever eaten. I would happily spend a lifetime on my knees if it means consuming her forever.

She rocks her hips against my hand, slow and sleepy. I unzip my jeans, take out my cock, and stroke myself in unison. Her body twitches from pleasure, the catalyst driving my own fulfilment as my fingers move faster, circling her clit, her breath shallow as she grinds against them in sheer desperation.

"That's it," I say. "Come for me, angel."

Shallow breaths become desperate whimpers. Her groans, low and addictive, are the sweetest sounds I've ever heard. She jerks against my hand, the crown slips from her head, and she comes undone all over my fingers.

My cock pulses, and I spill into my hands, my legs twitching as ribbons of cum spurt onto the grass.

Minutes pass. She stills. I lay with her until my final sunset. My perfect fit. My peaceful, dreaming doll.

Mine.

20

MILLIE

JUNE 22, 2012

My eyes flicker open, my fingertips gliding through blades of grass. Twilight cools the air, casting deep blue shadows over the atmosphere. I shiver, the absence of the sun giving me goosebumps, but it's still light enough to see. In the distance, the stone circle is illuminated with flickers of firelight. Music, chatter, and laughter vibrate through the ground.

A vague recollection of Zain's hand between my legs clouds my memory. I smile and reach out behind me, but I don't feel his presence. My brows furrow, and when I sit up and glance around, all I see is bruised grass and a wilted daisy chain, and I'm conscious that I'm all alone.

I know he was with me when I fell back to sleep. I sensed him, smelled him. His moans, the weight of his fingers, are still fresh in my memory. But I've never truly been in touch with reality—it's hard to know if it was all a dream. He wouldn't just leave me, would he?

At sunset, I start to weaken. His words in my head jolt me fully awake. I can't tell if it's just after sunset or just before sunrise. But if it's the latter, I'm too late.

Maybe he had a change of heart; perhaps I'm not what he wants. But I'm not going to jump to conclusions. Not when I have a chance to see this all play out. I try to remember who I was before all of this, and I can't. No matter how much I try and go back to her—myself—I can't. And I'm not sure that I want to. Too much has changed. But I'm not letting him pull a Trip Fontaine on me; I deserve more than that. And I can't wait six months for an answer. If he *has* deliberately left me here, I want to know why.

21

ZAIN

"Have you lost your fucking mind? You can't just leave the poor girl to fend for herself in the wilderness." Despite Sylvie's wrath, she welcomes me with a hug, sits me down and, after handing me a glass of water, checks my vital signs.

"That's what I said," Jasmine says.

"And me," Jesse pipes up.

"Me too," Josh says.

Solstice is a great night to die; it always has been. But with twilight come shadows that bring out the darker sides of all beings. I didn't want to leave Millie, but I couldn't stay. And my pride won't allow her to see me like this. Weak. Dependent. Subordinate. She'll never want me if she witnesses my transition. I wish I could have protected her from the beginning. But all I can do is hope that this journey has been enough and that she'll wait for me. I'm doing what's best for all of us.

By the time I've said my goodbyes to Jasmine and the twins, my vision is at around eighty percent. I go upstairs, shower, brush my teeth, dry my hair, get changed, and Sylvie hooks me up to an IV.

By the time the doorbell rings, my eyesight has deteriorated to around twenty percent.

And when I hear Millie's voice downstairs, I'm almost fully blind.

I'll never get used to losing my senses. All I can do now is lay in bed with the TV on for a bit of background noise.

I feel her presence right before her scent—forever imprinted on me—fills the room. My chest tightens. I haven't a clue how to play this, and now is not the time for games. I was too wrapped up in my selfishness and her perception of me to realise how much it would hurt her, given her past, to leave her all alone. I never should have abandoned her. The least I can do is apologise.

"I'm so sorry." My voice is strained, weak.

"For what? Leaving me out there to rot, or something else?" Her voice is distant, but it's hers. And maybe it's because I'm slowly losing my hearing, but it sounds like she's holding back from completely laying into me. And rightly so. I don't deserve her kindness.

I don't deserve her, period.

"For being a fucking coward. For everything." My voice is so quiet I can barely hear it. I clear my throat. "I didn't want you to see me like this." I pause. Now that she's here, I have a chance to put things right. "Millie... I want to tell you the truth about your mum."

She's quiet. Still. I strain my ears, but I can't hear any movement.

"Did you... did you know her?" she asks. I nod. "What was she like?" Her tone softens, and her scent grows stronger. Now that she's here, I need her close.

93

"She was a very special person." I smile, remembering the face that remarkably resembles Millie's. "Your mother's soul was destined to live many lifetimes. There was a fire inside of her that was far greater than herself, than anything in the mortal realm. Every time she completes a life cycle, her soul is reconditioned. Once she's served her purpose, she'll be free."

"You make her sound like some kind of superhero. No wonder she never wanted me."

I feel my way around the duvet cover, finding her fingers and threading them through mine, and she lets me. It's a relief to be touching her again. "Never think that. Of course, she wanted you. But she was troubled. Her mental illness made her believe that she wasn't good enough to be your mother. Sometimes, the spirit and the soul don't match up, and it creates chaos in the mind."

"Do you know where she is now?"

"I don't know if or when or where the souls are reborn. It's a lottery. All I know is they leave the underworld, and I don't see them again for a lifetime, sometimes less. And even then, I don't recognize their soul straightaway—because on the outside, they're a different person. Their human body isn't the same, although they usually bear some resemblance to the original."

She pauses, and for a while, all I can hear is her breathing. "I've never told anyone this, but when I found out the truth about how she died, I used to draw pictures of the two of us. When no one was around, I would set them alight and watch them burn. For a while, it helped me cope. It was cathartic. But I couldn't shake the guilt. I used to think I was a monster, that there was something wrong with me for carrying so much anger. For resenting her."

I squeeze her hand in an attempt to offer some comfort. "You're not a monster. Your feelings towards your mum are completely valid. You didn't hurt her; she hurt you. All this time, you've been trapped in a glass jar, suffocating, buried under all this guilt. The way you hate yourself so loudly... it's wasted you. Don't you think it's time you lift that lid and set yourself free?"

Her fingers sweep a strand of hair from my face and gently tuck it behind my ear. Gods, I already miss the way she touches me. I wish I could see her, comfort her. I wish I knew what she was thinking. "How am I going to do this without you?" No matter how hard she tries to mask the melancholy in her voice, I hear it.

"I promise you things will get easier. Don't think of it as a big chunk of time that needs to pass. Think of it like little bite-size pieces of time. One week. One day, one hour, if that's what you need.

"I'm not asking you to wait for me, but I'm asking you to try. When you get through the first week, try and complete the next week and the next. Keep doing it until the leaves turn orange, then brown. They'll fall and frost. The days will be shorter, colder, the nights longer, but I'll be here." I take the silver chain holding my spare house key from around my neck and give it to her. The brush of her fingers when she takes it is excruciating. "Stay at mine for as long as you like. Don't just exist in that time. Live. I promise you; every day will be a little easier. And then, once you've lived without me for a while, and you've learned to live for yourself, I'll be back again. Winter solstice...I'll come home."

Home. I've never looked at Earth like that before. I've never been in one place long enough to truly belong. But now, it feels right to call home to any dimension where she's with me.

"Zain?"

"Mm?"

"Thank you for finding me."

I smile. "You're welcome, Papillon."

She climbs onto my lap and kisses me, her soft, supple lips simultaneously soothing and driving me wild. This is all I've ever wanted. But not like this. Not when I'm hours from passing over. I taste the warm bitterness of tears, stinging, pacifying like saltwater on a wound. And suddenly, frustratingly, I hate myself. I hate that I've done this to her. I hate that my body is too weak to hold her the way I want to.

"I'm so sorry," I breathe.

"Shh," she says, pressing her body to mine. She smells like summer—earthy and sweet with the distinct scent of sun-exposed skin.

I part my lips, and her tongue glides softly against mine, our bodies tight, the closest we could ever be physically, yet not nearly close enough.

My hand slides up her back, pressing her closer, entrapping her for as long as I'm able to, while my other hand maps the softness of her curves, the rise and fall of her chest, the pounding of her heart, committing every part to memory. Her breath hitches as she grinds her hips, kissing me with more urgency, while I casually lose my mind in a kiss that's messy and chaotic and the sweetest thing I've ever tasted.

She's better than any dream. Better than life, better than death. Our body chemistry is a perfectly blended, perfectly balanced cocktail, and it's the only thing giving me life.

22

MILLIE

I want to curl into him and never let go.

"Penny for your thoughts?" he asks. I can tell he's trying to mask the pain, but I see it in his face every time he speaks, every time he moves. My chest tightens. I know it won't be long before he's gone.

"Can we just lay here?" I ask. It's a lot to take in for someone who has been alone their whole life, for someone who's been in the dark, to know how to navigate another person. And not just a person—a god. A god who just happens to be the lightest, most beautiful thing I've ever encountered. A god who belongs in the underworld—in the dark—yet manages to light up parts of my soul that in my twenty-three years I never believed possible. A soul that matches mine. That understands and accepts me in all my misery and darkness and doesn't try to change it.

In less than a day, we've gone from zero to sixty. In less than a day, I've gained someone who I want to hold onto forever. In less than a day, every negative thought I believed about myself and the world that has been cemented in my brain for as far back as I can remember has somehow ceased to exist. Because of Zain. And now it's all going to be taken away from me, and I have no idea what to do or how to feel.

And I hate myself for falling for someone so...unattainable. Almost as much as I used to hate myself.

I lay with him until his body stops holding me, his temperature falls, his beautiful face is drained of colour. And suddenly, frighteningly, I feel cold, like all life has been sucked out of me. Like I've lost a part of my soul. My mind goes hazy, and my vision blurs. I'm too scared to breathe because every breath I take is another second that he's not with me.

But breathing is all I have.

I don't know how long I lay there, but when I finally slip back into consciousness, it's light outside.

There's a knock on the door, and Jasmine enters. Her energy seems calmer than before. Softer. She's not a bad person, just a bad drunk, I think. I may forgive too easily, but I'm too tired, physically and mentally, to hold a grudge.

"We're heading off soon. Do you need a ride?" she asks, handing me a glass of water. I could easily drain a pint in one go, but I only take a small sip. I can still taste him, and I don't want anything to take away that small part of light and sweetness I have left of him in me.

"That would be great. Thank you."

I don't miss the lingering sadness when her gaze falls on Zain's lifeless body before she clears her throat and closes the door once again, leaving me alone with him. Maybe she loves him, too.

Love.

I wouldn't even know how that felt.

What are the chances of two people falling in love in less than two days? Lust? For sure. Obsession, infatuation, fascination, awe, longing. Sounds a lot like me. But love? Love is reserved for people who already love themselves.

Without him, I feel even less like me. Empty. Hollow. But it's a different kind of emptiness to the one I've always known. It's like I'd had a taste of something light, something freeing, and now that I'm without, it's even worse than before. I'm alive in the physical sense but not in my heart.

"Zain." I trace a finger along his jawline and commit those perfect angles of his face to memory. He looks peaceful—his features softened from sleep. He may look like a prince, but I sure as hell am not a princess. I know this isn't a fairy tale, and I'm not going to bring him back with true love's kiss. But I won't deny that he makes me feel things bigger than myself, like I'm bigger than myself. Six months is half a year too long to wait, yet I'd wait for him every year this way for the rest of forever if I had to. If this is the way it has to be, I'll wait.

Before my tears make tracks, I wipe them away. I seldom cry because it's so rare for me to feel any emotion, but it feels right to now because I'm completely and irrevocably overwhelmed with gratitude for this man. Even though I know he can't hear me, I say it anyway because a part of me needs to hear it out loud too. I whisper, "Thank you for giving me a chance at life." I bring his hand to my lips and kiss the tips of his fingers. Then I smooth the hair from his face.

And I let him go.

23

MILLIE

JUNE 23, 2012

It's been less than twenty-four hours since I've been warm. Zain's flat feels like a sauna, yet inside I'm cold as ice. Now I've had a taste of warmth, I'm colder than I've ever been. I've been spoiled by him in every way, and now it's a waiting game. A little less than six months.

That's all.

I can't face going home yet; I can't leave this place. Not when everything reminds me of him. When I run myself a bath in an attempt to get myself warm, I try to memorise the signature cocktail of herbs and oils Zain uses, but it doesn't smell the same. Nothing is the same apart from the fading scent of him filling this place. And no amount of wizardry can replicate that smell. His scent belongs solely to him.

I give up on the bath; I don't have the energy or the motivation to wash. Instead, I make a bed on the living room floor and wrap myself in his scent. I know that he's nowhere on or buried in this earth, but if I can visualise that this other dimension he's in is only a few feet underground, if I try to be as close as I can, then it might make this easier. And if being on the floor keeps me that little bit closer to him, then this is where I'll stay until I'm able to muster the energy to move, to leave his place and go home, or until he comes back to me—whichever comes first. And God, I hope it isn't the latter. Don't get me wrong, there's nothing I want more than to see his face right now, but I hope that I can heal enough to drag myself up and dust myself off and piece myself together before he finds me like this. Pathetic, but not broken. Not anymore. I won't allow it. Not when I know that he's waiting for me. Not when I have someone to live for.

It's dark outside when I tune into a noise other than my own thoughts; the sound of a car's engine cutting outside. And my heart jumpstarts when I hear a key turn in the lock of the front door.

The first thing I see is a mass of hair shoved up into a messy bun and the small, slim silhouette of a woman. She's wearing dark jeans and a black hoodie, at least that's what I think she's wearing—it's hard to see through the dark and fatigue.

"Jasmine?" I manage to croak. It's the first time I realise how dry my throat is.

My outburst makes her jolt. "Millie? You scared me. I didn't realise you were still here," she says.

"Neither did I," I quietly muse, leaving out the part where I feel like my soul has left my body. But, like Zain, my physical form is still earthbound. I'm glad she doesn't ask any questions.

"I um...I come here to check on the place when Zain...goes away. You know, take out the bins, give everything a wipe over, empty the fridge, that sort of thing. Makes things easier for him when he gets back." I say nothing, yet she continues. "It takes a lot of energy to transition between worlds."

How would *she* know? Clearly, I'm still a little pissed. Or maybe it's because hunger has reared its head.

"Are you...are you like him?" I ask.

She shakes her head. "No."

"Jasmine?"

"Yes."

"Do you love him?" I regret saying it the moment I ask. I don't want to know the answer.

"I did, once," she says, sitting down on the couch. The couch where he finger-fucked me into submission. But that was all a fantasy. "It was a long time ago. Almost half a century, in fact."

"What are you?"

"I'm a dryad—a wood nymph. We don't live as long as gods."

"Oh. That explains a lot." Like the reason she's one of the most beautiful people I've ever seen. "And Jesse and Josh?"

"Satyrs. Like me. We live in the forest, usually, but we've always served Zain. Us three, and whoever Sylvie's place gets passed down to. It's no coincidence that she became our foster parent." She clears her throat and checks her watch. "Anyway, I'd better get a move on. I'll come back soon to sort out the house. Make sure you get some rest...on a proper bed," she says, side-eyeing the floor I'm still lying on.

I flash her a small smile, and she gives me one last glance before she leaves, pulling the door behind her and signalling another round of excruciating, deathly silence.

Time passes, and I'm still cocooned in the duvet. But my body still feels like December. Empty. Hollow. Freezing cold without a sign of life.

The only thing I feel is tired.

More time passes, slowly and without warning, while I drift in and out of sleep until I wake up shaking without any recollection of a dream or nightmare. It's like my body is rejecting the solitude. Like it knows that our loneliness is unsustainable.

It knows we need Zain to live. Six months without him is going to kill me for sure, but I guess I have to try.

Golden sunlight streams through a gap in the curtain. My tummy rumbles, and my bladder contracts, signalling its fullness. My brain leads my body in a slow crawl to the bathroom, where I empty it, then return back to the paralysing numbness in my spot on the floor.

Then I wait.

It's all I can do to wait and listen for that key to turn in the lock.

It doesn't today. In fact, I wait for that sound every day. I wait until I tire of keeping track of the sun. And I pray for darkness. Because I know that every time night falls upon me, I'm one day closer to seeing Zain again. The days are so long now that one day feels like forever.

I'm left wondering if Jasmine will come at all. Or if she assumes I'll clean up this place. Maybe she pities me so much that she can't bear to be in the same vicinity. That she's probably keeping an eye on the place, waiting for me to leave. But the longer I'm here—the less this place smells like him, *feels* like him—the harder it is to leave.

Night falls. It's quiet, but my body won't let me sleep. My throat hurts, and there's a throbbing in my head that won't quit. I contemplate suicide on too many occasions to count; I'm desperate. But there's no guarantee I'll end up in Summerland with Zain. And even if I did, would I feel the same about him in another dimension? Would I feel anything at all?

I sit with my unanswered questions and the certainty that he'll be back here by Christmas, but that's still six long months away. In six months, I'll be a corpse if I stay here and let myself rot.

When I finally manage to peel myself off the floor, I secure the duvet around me once again, every inch of my body aching as it gets accustomed to movement, before I help myself to a glass of water.

I drain half the liquid and throw the rest away—I won't allow myself to have any more than the bare minimum of what I need. Self-harm in the form of abstinence is the only way that makes sense to me right now in order to get through this. A cry for help from the gods to bring me *my* god—no matter the price. I stumble onto the couch and press my middle finger between my brows—a trick I've learned to alleviate the tension in my head—but the ache is far too strong to be cured by touch.

I close my eyes, but the silence is so loud that it makes sleep impossible—as if sleep is even an option right now. My brain is restless and has other ideas. I sigh audibly, my irritation startling me because it's the first emotion I've felt other than sadness in days. In a way, it's nice to not feel like I'm festering, rotting on a floor, waiting to die.

I glance around the room, and for the first time since I've been here, I notice things again. Objects, books, the altar, that creepy looking ram skull. Zain's music collection.

Music. The only acceptable way to feel close to him. A safer way than being in a state of starvation or dehydration, or being drunk or high, or cutting my wrists in a bathtub to experience the euphoric lightness of crossing over into another dimension.

For so long, all I've ever wanted in my heart was to be in that otherworld, in my mother's safety, but right now, the only thing I want is to feel Zain with me again. Here on Earth.

I slip Ocean Rain out of its sleeve and place it on the record player. It takes me a few tries to get the needle on the right song, but when The Killing Moon starts to play, I'm instantly transported to the night we met, back when I was years younger than I am now.

Although I know exactly what I'm looking for, I browse every book on the bookshelf, running my fingertips along each spine, absorbing his energy through the volumes until I reach one called *Celtic Gods and Myths*. If I can't see him in reality, at least there's another way.

I open the book and thumb through, pausing every now and again when I come across something I find interesting, but it's not engaging enough to hold my attention. Not when I know I'm pages from seeing Zain's face.

Finally, I see him. And it's almost like the time spent in his company had made me forget just how beautiful he is. Because I'm completely in awe, amazed that somebody could be so breath-taking.

Heart-stopping.

If the image is an accurate depiction, his immortal body is a broader, wider, taller version of his human form. Facially, he bears similarities; his eyes are identical. His perfect jawline is partly hidden under a long, pointed beard, and his hair is much longer. Waves and braids fall over his chest and shoulders, right down to his waist, and he wears a crown of leaves and foliage with stag-like horns and a simple gold torc around his neck. In the image, he has no body art like his human form. Instead, he's surrounded by every animal he usually wears in ink. Butterflies, ravens, stags, and a horned serpent—each one almost identical to his tattoos.

Then I see the name of the illustrator. Jasmine Moreau. And it all falls into place.

And I know now that I can never compete with her. She's been with him since the beginning. He has her ink on him. Her art. Her soul.

I close the book and return it to its home on the shelf.

I'm not even sad, not really. Because now I know, and now I can set out with what I was supposed to do three days ago. This little blip has cemented everything I thought I knew about the world—that people will use you for their own gain. That nobody cares, and *nobody* understands, or ever will. Just like my mother, I'm not meant for this world, and this world isn't meant for me. So, if I meet Zain in the afterlife, the underworld, Summerland—whatever the hell it's called—then so be it. I'll be ready. At least I can take away the fact that I got some decent orgasms under my belt before I die.

I've never felt so awake. So conscious. So in tune with my body and my own needs. Maybe this is the wake-up call I need. And now I'm suddenly aware of the fact that I stink to high heaven and of the ache in my body from lying lifeless on the floor for so long.

I change the record to something a little more current, a little punchier, and run the bath, filling it with aromatherapy oils and Epsom salts and all the other wonderful smelling potions Zain has hiding in a bathroom cupboard. When I find a razor, I stare at it for a few seconds, hesitating before I grab it and put it on the side of the tub. I shave my legs and wash my hair. All the while, I'm hyperaware of how easy it would be to end things right here, right now. I'd know how to do it properly this time. But things have changed. Too much has changed, and a long soak in the bath isn't going to undo all the work that's been done these past few days. I need to learn myself again, but it's not to say that if I choose to stay alive, I won't choose to reunite with Zain at winter solstice.

Once I'm finished, I throw on a clean pair of shorts and a t-shirt, brush my teeth, clean the bath, and bag up all my dirty clothes ready to take with me. I don't want to leave any trace of my being here when he or Jasmine returns. But when I go to leave, my vision blurs, and then it's black.

When I come around, the room is pitch dark, and it takes me a minute to gain awareness of my surroundings, as well as recognise that I'm still in Zain's apartment, lying on his floor, with a plastic bag filled with dirty clothes by my side. And I realise then that the only thing I forgot to do was eat.

After a few attempts, I manage to pull myself up off the floor and into the kitchen. There isn't a lot of choice in the fridge, but I manage to make something without too much effort; a couple of boiled eggs and some berries that are past their best. That will fuel me enough to bring me home.

Once I've washed up, dried, tidied, and triple-checked everything is turned off, I take one last glance at the place I called home for a short and bittersweet time.

Goodbye, Zain.

Back to my old life I go.

24

ZAIN

JUNE 23, 2012

Something's wrong.

It's dark. My eyes are closed. At least I assume they are. Everything hurts when I try to move. My ribcage feels like it's stuck in one place. It hurts to breathe.

"Zain?" I try to recognise the voice, but it sounds like it's travelling through water. "Zain, can you hear me, darling?"

Then I realise they're calling my Earth name. Not Cernunnos. And I realise then that something must have gone wrong during the transition. The changeover is never usually seamless, but this has never happened to me before.

A small circle of warmth sits in the centre of my chest. I embrace it, visualise it expanding, and it works as an anchor to aid my breathing. With every moment, my ribcage swells. Each passing painful breath eases the tightness in my chest until I can breathe freely, and I drift back out of consciousness.

The next time I wake, I'm treated to the sound of that voice again. It's still blurred, but I can make out the sound of singing. For a moment, I mistake the voice for my mothers. But it can't be—I've not heard that sound for millennia. I must be dreaming.

Suddenly the sound grows closer. Clearer. And I recognise sweet Sylvie's voice—she's singing the song she uses to bring me around—Earth Angel, a favourite of mine from the '50s. It always amazes me that music holds such power. All these years, she's looked after me out of the kindness of her own heart—she's always been like a mother to me.

But why am I here?

I'm far too weak to make a sound louder than a whimper. So, I wait. And I silently pray that Millie's okay. For her sake and mine.

Time passes, and again I try to speak, but it still hurts. All I can do is breathe, slow and steady. And think of her.

25

MILLIE

JUNE 28, 2012

I don't know how I got here.

That's the messed-up thing about dissociation—one minute, I'm in one place, and the next? I'm sitting on a beach with a plastic bag of dirty clothes beside me, holding onto my mum's tarot cards. Again.

I don't know what fucking day it is, but I could guess by the stubble on my legs that it's been a couple of days since I left Zain's apartment.

God, I miss him. I really do. And I know now that my reaction to Jasmine's illustrations was some sort of trauma response. I overreacted. Or rather, my intrusive thoughts did.

I check my phone; it's dead. I make a mental note to find a charging point so I can check in with work—although I'm pretty sure they'd sack me on the spot if I tried to come back now. In all honestly, I'm not sure I'd want to go back. Too much has changed for me to number crunch all day long or endure mediocre small talk with colleagues who think I'm weird or drink crappy cups of instant coffee from a kettle that needs constant descaling.

In a strange turn of events, I find myself wanting to give life a chance. And though I may not know which path to take, I'm willing to find one. Just like Persephone, I need to reject this victim mentality I've carried with me my entire life and move beyond my power. I need to embrace who I truly am.

I need to feel what Zain has made me feel every day since I met him. Sparks, fire, excitement, warmth, comfort, safety. I never knew I could crave somebody so deeply. His touch, his energy, his soul. I never knew someone could make me feel the sun from the inside out, and I'll never be satisfied until I have him again. Everything else just isn't enough.

The ocean calls to me like a siren's song, strong and gentle as a lullaby, luring me in to be held. Slowly, I peel off my clothes, stripping down to my underwear, and I leave them in a pile next to the bag of dirty ones. Then I hotfoot over the shingled shoreline to the lip of the ocean.

I immerse myself in the cold depths and swim out until my feet can no longer reach the bottom, and I float, laying there like a starfish, letting the waves lap over me. I'd forgotten how nice it feels to be held. Soothed. Comforted. Wanted. The way Zain makes me feel. It feels like the last time he held me was such a long time ago.

The water takes me, rocking me slowly towards the horizon, and I allow my thoughts to drift to him. My Zain. My anchor and my harbour. And in my head, I replay the night we met, and every moment since in super speed. Only I didn't know that they were perfect moments when they were present. It's funny how we romanticise nostalgia; people never realise what's important when it's staring them in the face.

Every damn moment with him has been perfect, and if I have to spend six months reliving them until I get him back, then so be it. And now all I want is to live. For him. For me. For my mum. And I know it's going to be hard, but I owe this to myself. And if, for whatever reason, it doesn't work out, I'll know I tried.

I'm too far gone in my thoughts to realise the distance I've drifted. The ocean grips me. I try to move, to roll onto my back, but I go nowhere. My legs make tracks underwater like I'm climbing a Stairmaster, weakened within moments. Then suddenly, forcefully, she pulls me under.

Natural instinct kicks in. I hold my breath, resisting the urge to inhale, and fight to break the surface and take the breaths I've taken for granted all these years. But I'm not sure how long I can keep it up. This is nothing like how I imagined, submerged in a place that is suffocating and the furthest thing from peaceful.

In my head, my body is still rooting for me, but my lungs don't get the memo. I breathe in, and the water comes rushing in, burning my chest, making me cough and splutter, but there's no reprieve. It hurts. Everything hurts. Fear compresses my chest in a vice-like grip as water floods my lungs.

Unbearable pain rips through me as pressure builds inside my head, my brain throbbing, my heart pounding inside my ears, thumping through my chest as the realisation hits me. I'm going to die.

Suddenly, it's quiet. The pain subsides. I can breathe.

I look up. The surface is in my grasp.

But then I see her. My mum. The calm amidst the chaos. The only light in the darkness. And it's like looking in a mirror.

She's so much more beautiful than the photos I have of her. Ethereal, like a goddess. It has me wondering if this is the way Zain sees me.

I'm overwhelmed with emotion. This is everything I wanted, yet now I've had a taste of what life could be like, it's the last thing I want.

She reaches for me, holding out her hand. Her presence is serene, magnetic, bathed in a light that makes her look like a divine being.

This is what I needed. Clarity. Closure. Euphoria. To be physically close to the person whose body I once inhabited, to hear her heartbeat once again, see her smile, to smell her. It's bittersweet that this is how it all ends.

Finally, as though accepting the fate I've known all along, I reach for her. When she takes my hand, I tremble.

Then it all goes dark.

26

MILLIE

JUNE 30, 2012

"Wake up, sleepyhead."

I would know Zain's voice anywhere. In any lifetime, any universe, any dimension.

"Is this Summerland?" I ask, groggily. My head is throbbing, my mouth devoid of moisture. Swallowing feels like broken glass.

He laughs, but it's hollow. "You can't get away from me that easily, Papillon. You're in the hospital."

My eyes flutter open. After taking a moment to adjust to the bright, artificial lights, I'm treated to his devastatingly beautiful face. My chest swells. God, I've missed him.

"Millie, there's something you need to know." His eyes glaze over, bloodshot and raw, with dark circles underneath like he hasn't slept in days. "You died."

The last twenty-four hours flash through my memory. "I wasn't trying to kill myself," I blurt out. It hurts like hell to speak, but I need him to know the truth.

"I know," he says, brushing the hair from my face. All I can do is lean into his touch. "I was so scared I'd lost you."

"Did you... did you save me?"

He nods. "Who knew I had a saviour complex, right?"

"How are you here?"

"Well, it turns out the underworld don't take kindly to gods who fall in love with mortals." He tells me the story of how he was banished from the underworld for breaking the rules, but I'm barely listening. He loves me? Everything he's ever known has ceased to exist because of me, and he seems completely unphased by it all.

"Zain? Are... are you okay?" I ask when he's finished.

"I'm perfect. Don't you see? Both of us were trapped, stagnant in our worlds. Staying still, never moving forward. I never had any excitement—any plans—for the future. My only goal was you. I wanted to know you. I wanted to know... what you felt like." He pins me with his gaze. It's brighter, clearer than before, like someone's picked out the prettiest pieces of the sky and placed them in his eyes. They still have that same heart-stopping effect on me. "And then I got to feel you, and taste you, and fuck you. I got to breathe you, see your light grow. When I thought I'd lost you, the otherworld stopped making sense. I finally understood why I couldn't let you die for the past nine years. I'm hopelessly, irrevocably, *endlessly,* addicted to you."

He's always been impossibly beautiful, but like this, with the sun beaming through the panes of glass behind him, he looks otherworldly, like some kind of angel, and I'm thankful that he saved me. That he's with me. That he loves me. And I hope to God I'm not dreaming.

"I may no longer be a god, but you will always be my goddess."

"But what about the underworld?"

He shrugs as if the duties he's had for thousands of years haven't just fallen completely flat. "It's a job for the moon goddess, now."

"Why are you so casual about this?"

"Because, Papillon, of all the ways I've seen mortals die, ours will be the most heavenly, the most epic, of all." He reaches into his back pocket, pulls something out, and hands it to me. It's the tarot card he took from me, crumpled and beaten by saltwater. "The two of cups. It reflects intimacy, tenderness, reverence, soulmates, twin flames... reunification. It's you and me, Pet."

A shadow shields the sun as Zain's mouth descends onto mine. His kiss is unlike the others. Gentle. Soft. Patient. And somehow, I know that this kiss means more than any other I've ever had. This is the one I'll remember forever. *This* is how kissing somebody should always feel. Like safety, warmth, and comfort. Life-giving. Healing. This is the start of a second chance for both of us to start anew. The first day of our lives.

"Zain?" I say against his mouth.

"Mmm?"

"I think I messed up, too."

"You do? And why is that?" The mirth in his smile indicates that he knows exactly what I'm about to confess.

"I never needed saving; I just needed to be found. Maybe I don't know how to love, but I'm more than willing to learn. I'm in so deep that being with you feels like drowning and floating, all at the same time. You helped me find my way in the dark. And I'm terrified that I might not be everything you want, but I'm ready to dive into the fear if it means chasing every sunrise with you."

His smile widens before he lays a sweet, gentle kiss on the top of my head, then he climbs onto the bed and holds me.

Three days ago, forever seemed like the worst kind of torture. Now it doesn't seem like long enough. And I want nothing more than to spend my years with him.

"What do you mortals do for fun anyway?" he asks.

I smile because I know exactly where he's going with this. "I'm sure we can think of a few things."

"Is that so?" He pulls me closer, and I nestle into the chest that holds the most precious thing that belongs to me—his wonderful, beating, human heart. It's a feeling I'll never let go of for as long as I live, and if it's with him, I can only hope it will last a lifetime.

ACKNOWLEDGMENTS

First and foremost, I would like to thank all of my beautiful readers for picking up this book. There are so many great stories out there, so I am deeply honoured and humbled that you have chosen to read mine.

To Ria, thank you for designing such a beautiful cover—I am forever in awe of your magic. I cannot wait to work with you again.

To Charlie, thank you for being such a wonderful editor. You are such a pleasure to work with.

To JL Peridot, Sarah Smith, Skye McDonald, and Stefanie Simpson. My kindred spirits, my sisters-from-other-misters, thank you for all your advice, your support, your kindness, and your guidance. I don't know what I'd do without you. I love you from the bottom of my heart.

S, thank you for being one of the good ones. I don't know where I'd be without you. I love you endlessly.

A, my number one for life. Thank you for being the most precious, sweet and funny little guy. I love you behind my back, always.

To my family, thank you for accepting, loving, and supporting me—fucked-up parts and all—on this wild journey. I love you to the stars and beyond.

To anyone else who has helped and supported me—ARC readers, bookstagrammers, booktokers, and more...THANK YOU!

Finally, to Steph, Chris, and all the ones we've lost to mental illness; I hope you've found your peace. And to the ones left behind; you are warriors. This book is for you.

If you or anyone you know is struggling with mental health issues, please don't be afraid to reach out to your local organisation. Your mental health matters.

UK Charities to support:
Mind *www.mind.org.uk*
CALM *www.thecalmzone.net*
Shout *www.giveusashout.org*

Also By Sonia Palermo

Hot Girl Summer

ABOUT AUTHOR

Sonia Palermo is a writer of New Adult Gothic and Contemporary Romance. She lives in a village on the south coast of England with her partner and son. She loves books, coffee, horror films, and the ocean.

You can find Sonia Palermo on these social platforms:

Twitter → @sonia_palermo
Instagram → @sonia_palermo_
Goodreads → Sonia Palermo

Printed in Great Britain
by Amazon

24372030R00078